MISTLETOE MINE

AN ETERNITY SPRINGS HOLIDAY NOVELLA

ETERNITY SPRINGS

EMILY MARCH

EMILY MARCH
BOOKS

Mistletoe Mine
An Eternity Springs Novella
Emily March

Mistletoe Mine is a work of fiction. Names, characters, places, and incidents are the products of the author's imagination or are used fictitiously. Any resemblance to actual events, locales, or persons, living or dead, is entirely coincidental.

Published in the United States by Emily March Books

ISBN 978-1-942002-65-9 (digital)

ISBN 978-1-942002-66-6 (print)

PART I

August
Eternity Springs, Colorado

Molly Stapleton stood in the middle of the footbridge spanning Angel Creek and watched a green leaf from a cottonwood tree drift on the swirling breeze. It floated up, then down and around before a downdraft deposited the heart-shaped leaf on the surface of the icy mountain stream. The current swept it toward the bank and into a miniature whirlpool, where it circled three times before shooting out to cling to a mist-bathed stone. Moments later, a crash of froth knocked it loose, tossing the leaf into a bubbling, churning stretch of white water.

At this point in her life, Molly could identify with the leaf.

One week before classes began for her final semester of college, she was in the rock-clinging rest period. Barring a stumble in the upper-level statistics class that worried her, she would graduate in December with a business degree from Texas A&M University. Behind her swirled the eddy of her collegiate years. She'd loved her time as an undergrad, and she hated to think this time of her life would soon be over. Part of Leaf-Molly wanted to slip off the stone and work her way back to that pool, where she'd found peace and sanctuary away from the turbulence of her imploding family.

Even as she yearned for the familiar comfort of the past, she looked forward to leaping today into the churning white water of life after college. The rapids ahead promised thrills and excitement. A new career. A new home. New people in her life.

Which brought her thoughts to Mason. Mason Malone, whom she'd dated since her sophomore year. Would he be her white-water guide, or were they destined to travel two different creek branches after college?

Molly didn't know where Mason stood on the matter of marriage. They'd only talked about a possible future in vague, general terms. True, she'd sent him mixed messages about her opinion of marriage depending on whether she'd recently spoken with one of her parents. Still, he hadn't seemed all that anxious to bring up the subject himself, either.

Stop it, she scolded herself. She shouldn't let concerns about the future cloud her enjoyment of today. This was resting-on-the-rock time, after all. She and Mason had spent a fabulous morning with their group of college friends biking the Alpine Loop above Eternity Springs. When Mason had asked to spend some time alone with her this afternoon, she'd quickly agreed. They had a picnic date, and she intended to enjoy it.

"Hello, beautiful."

Molly turned at the welcome sound of Mason Malone's voice. "Hey, handsome. You're early."

"So are you," he replied, his grin just a little bashful as he approached the bridge from the direction of Cavanaugh House, the main structure on the grounds of Angel's Rest Healing Center and Spa, the resort where their group was staying.

Molly's heart turned over at his smile. Mason was tall, with a lean, lanky build, sun-bleached hair, and eyes that reminded her of a mountain forest—deep green with flecks of gold and brown. He was an engineering student at A&M, a small-town boy whose polite manners and gentle nature sometimes reminded her of her father. She was head-over-heels in love with Mason.

"Are you hungry?" he asked, calling her attention to the picnic basket he carried in his right hand.

"Starved," she replied. "Vacationing is hard work."

"Tell me about it," Mason replied. "This altitude has me huffing and puffing like a flatlands boy."

"You are a flatlands boy," Molly pointed out.

"True. A flatlands boy and"—he reached for her hand, then leaned down to give her a slow, thorough kiss—"a hungry man."

The look in his eyes told her he wasn't thinking about sandwiches. Molly played with the top button of his green checkered sport shirt. "Just how private is this picnic spot you've picked out?"

"Not private enough, I'm afraid," he said, giving a rueful sigh. "I should have planned better." But after a ten-minute, hand-in-hand walk through the rose garden at Angel's Rest, he led her to a grassy spot beside the creek where it was apparent that he'd planned perfectly.

A beautiful double wedding ring quilt stitched in shades of autumn lay spread across the ground. One of her favorite songs played softly from a small wireless speaker sitting off to one side. At one corner of the quilt sat a glass ice bucket, two crystal champagne flutes, and a tall, clear vase filled with a dozen red roses. "Oh, wow." Then her brow creased in worry. "Did I forget a special occasion?"

"Every day with you is a special occasion."

"Oh, Mason." She rolled her eyes, but her heart went warm and gooey inside. "Everything is so lovely. You've gone to so much trouble."

"I wanted our picnic to be perfect."

Molly glanced around. The forest, the perfume of roses on the air, their song blended with the music of the bubbling creek, majestic mountain peaks rising beyond the valley. "It is perfect, Mason."

"Wait until you see what we have to eat. I got your favorite."

"Chicken salad sandwiches from the Mocha Moose?" Molly had enjoyed everything she'd ordered at the small coffee-and-sandwich shop in town, but their chicken salad topped her list.

"No." He set the picnic basket beside the flowers, took her into his arms, and kissed her so sweetly that Molly's knees went weak. "PB and J. With toasted bread, crunchy peanut butter, and elderberry jam."

"Elderberry! I can't believe they had that in the little grocery store here."

"I came prepared. I brought it with me from home. I bought the bread from the Mocha Moose, but I toasted the bread and made the sandwiches myself. I sweet-talked Celeste Blessing into letting me use Angel's Rest's kitchen."

She laughed out loud. "My hero!"

He hesitated, then asked, "Am I?"

"My hero? Yes, definitely. You are always there for me. You always know exactly what I need."

"I hope so. I hope I've read you right."

His voice sounded tight. Molly sensed a change in the mood of the moment, and she stared at him intently.

Mason cleared his throat. "I was going to wait until after the picnic to do this, but the suspense is about to kill me." His smile went a little shaky, and he took both her hands in his. "Mary Elizabeth Stapleton, I love you. I love your warm and generous heart. I love your silly jokes. I love that wicked smart brain of yours. I love the way you complete me. You are the most beautiful woman in the entire world, not just because you blow right past ten on the hotness scale, but because of who you are inside, too."

"Oh, Mason." That was the sweetest thing any guy had ever said to her. "I love you, too. I—"

"No. Let me finish. We both have big changes in front of us. Lots of big decisions to make. I know we haven't talked about this much and that you are gun-shy because of your parents' split. Still, I've analyzed all the data, and I think we'll be happier in the long term if we make these decisions together."

Molly melted inside. Her beloved engineer was such a nerd sometimes.

But then he dropped down on one knee and caused Molly's heart to thunder. She steepled her hands over her mouth and waited.

Mason pulled a black velvet ring box from his pants pocket and opened it to reveal a sparkling solitaire set in a platinum band. "Molly, will you marry me?"

Marry. *Mason wants to marry me.* She'd dreamed about this possibility. She thought she wanted to be Molly Malone more than just about anything. Yet, here at the moment of truth, a ribbon of uncertainty fluttered through her. Her parents had once been head-over-heels in love. Look at them now? Look at all the pain they'd experienced. The pain that *she'd* experienced. What if—?

Then Mason, because he *was* Mason and knew her

so well, loved her so much, said the words she needed to hear. "Be brave, Molly. Believe in us. I do."

"You do?"

"I do. Marry me."

Yes. Yes! She could do this. She would do this. She wouldn't make the same mistakes her mother and father had made. She threw herself into Mason's arms. "Yes. Yes, I'll marry you. I love you, Mason. I want to marry you and make a home with you and someday have your babies."

"Thank God. Me, too. Except…emphasis on 'someday' in regards to those babies," he clarified. "Not right away. Right?"

"Right." She laughed. "We have plenty of time for babies. Besides, I want you all to myself for a while."

"I want that, too. I also want kids. But before we have them, we'll need to buy a house and build up a 401K and college savings account. We haven't talked about children very much, either. How many do you think you'll want? If we want more than two and with optimal spacing between pregnancies, we should—"

"Kiss. Kiss me, Mason." Molly planted her mouth on Mason's, and for a time, the passion of the present erased all thoughts of the future from their minds.

Eventually, broke apart, poured the champagne, and dove into the peanut butter and jelly sandwiches. The conversation returned to their future, their hopes and wishes and dreams. When he mentioned how thrilled his parents would be about the engagement, Molly thought about her mom and dad.

A gray cloud drifted across her sunshine sky. She glanced down at the sparkling ring on the third finger of her left hand. Sadness and a measure of anger rippled through her. She wanted to share her big news with the people she loved the most—her parents.

But her parents weren't together, so she couldn't share her news with them in a single call. She had to choose which parent to call first. Whoever she didn't call first would have their feelings hurt. Oh, they wouldn't say it aloud, but she'd know it. She would feel guilty.

She shouldn't have to feel guilty today. Not about this. The fact that she would feel guilty torqued her. At significant moments like this, the sorry state of her family broke her heart.

"What's wrong?" Mason asked, his brow knitting in a frown. "You've gone all stiff. What's the matter? You don't like the ring? You said you liked the ring!"

"I love the ring," Molly assured him. She smiled up into his worried eyes. "I love you."

"Then why do you have a look on your face like somebody canceled Christmas?"

She shook her head. She wouldn't talk about Mom and Dad. This was a moment for marriage, not divorce. "I'm sorry. I'm just feeling emotional. This is an emotional time for a girl."

"You're thinking about your mom, aren't you? I can always tell. Want to call her? I'll bet we could find a decent cell signal with a little effort."

"No. Not now. She's in London. It'll be late over there."

"Your dad, then?"

"No. I'm fine, really. I have you. I don't need anyone but you. You've made me just so happy, Mason."

"Then don't cry. Please?" He tucked an errant strand of her auburn hair behind her ear. "I hate it when you cry."

"I'm not crying." She blinked away tears.

His frown deepened. "And don't try to give me that nonsense about happy tears. Tears are tears, Molly, and I don't like 'em. Seeing you cry gives me heartburn, and I left my antacids in the pocket of my jeans."

Molly smiled at him lovingly. Her nerdy engineering grad student rarely wore anything other than jeans, but he'd dressed in khaki slacks to propose. His effort touched her. Other guys went to elaborate lengths to create big events out of their marriage proposals. By keeping it simple and private and beautiful, Mason had done it just right and made it a perfect moment.

Well, almost perfect. He couldn't do anything about her folks. But Molly had a BFF who was right here in town. Joyous excitement burned away the remnants of her tears. "Let's go find Lori and share the news with her. She's going to be so excited."

"Um . . ." Mason rubbed the back of his neck, his grin turning sheepish. "About Lori. She sorta already knows."

"You told her?" Molly folded her arms and tried to

look dismayed, though he looked so darned guiltily cute that she doubted she pulled it off.

He was quick to explain. "I wasn't about to choose a ring you will wear for the rest of your life without doing the research. Since Lori is your roommate and best friend, I figured she'd be the one to ask for help. She gave me suggestions about the diamond's style and cut, but I didn't show it to her, Molly."

"I wouldn't have cared if you had. I'm glad you asked Lori. It's exactly the ring I've always wanted."

"Well, good."

"Does she know you were going to propose this afternoon?"

"No." He scowled in affront. "This was private, just for you and me."

He's so perfect for me. "I love you, Mason Malone."

"I love you, too, Molly-Stapleton-soon-to-be-Molly-Malone." He hesitated, then asked, "You will take my name, won't you? So, we won't have the hyphen thing going on?"

"No hyphen thing." She gave him a playful kiss on the mouth.

Mason, being Mason, took it from playful to passionate, and when they finally broke apart, he spoke with strain in his voice. "Honey, I think we probably better move to a more public place, unless"—he shot her a hopeful look—"you want to find a private spot?"

"Later," she promised, happiness rushing through her. "It's almost three-thirty now. Lori and I planned to meet at four and shop for last-minute bargains before the Christmas in August festival closes. Want to tag along?"

"Sure. I need to be there at five, anyway, because I promised Celeste I'd help her break down the Angel's Rest booth." He stole one more quick kiss, then reaffirmed, "Later."

They held hands while walking from Angel's Rest to the center of Eternity Springs. This was Molly's second visit to the little Colorado mountain town home of her college roommate, Lori Reese. Despite being three years older, Molly had become fast friends with Lori when they'd both worked at the university bookstore the previous year. Lori had walked into the stockroom one afternoon to find Molly crying following a phone call with her dad. They'd shared absentee-father stories and bonded while restocking racks of T-shirts.

Molly had adored Eternity Springs when she first visited the previous summer. Celeste Blessing called the town a little piece of heaven, and Molly agreed. She'd been delighted to return this year for ten days between the end of summer school and the start of the fall semester. Celeste had cut them a super-cheap deal on rooms at Angel's Rest. Lori's mom had supplied them with most of their meals. That Mason had managed to rearrange his work schedule and make the trip up to the mountains for eight days, too, made it the best of vacations.

The three-day Christmas in August event added to the small town's charm. Holiday trimmings decorated the streets, and Molly could almost believe it was

Christmas with the scent of roasting chestnuts and the songs of strolling carolers drifting in the air. Well, Christmas in Texas, anyway, where it could be a balmy sixty-five degrees in December. She recalled that Lori had said that last year on Christmas Day, the thermometer had topped out at a frigid five degrees in Eternity Springs. Today the beautiful August weather had brought the tourists out in droves. For Molly, seeing so many families enjoying the festive atmosphere was bittersweet. Her family quit vacationing together years ago.

Molly saw Lori seated on the bench in the park where they'd planned to meet. Lori spied the ring before Molly even had a chance to show it off, and her squeals of delight all but drowned out "We Wish You a Merry Christmas" coming from a nearby trio. "It's gorgeous," Lori said. "Oh, Mason. You did a fabulous job."

"Didn't he?" Molly beamed up at her fiancé. Her fiancé. She clasped the word to her heart. She had a fiancé! "He tells me you gave him guidance, so props to you, bestie."

Eyes twinkling, Lori blew on her knuckles and brushed them against her shoulder.

Lori then launched into a series of wedding plans questions for which Molly had no answers. Finally, laughing, she looped her arm through her roommate's and said, "Enough! Nothing has been decided about our wedding. We've barely had time to discuss it. Once we get things figured out, I promise you'll be one of the first to know. After all, as my maid of honor, you'll need to have all of the intel."

"Maid of honor? Me?"

"Of course, you. If you'll do me the honor, that is. I want you…no, I need you…in that role. I'll do an official bridesmaid invitation once we get some of the wedding details nailed down, but please, Lori. Will you be my MOH?"

"Yes. I'd love to be your MOH. Oh, thank you, Molly. I'm going to cry!"

"Don't cry," Molly said.

"Don't cry," Mason repeated. "Crying women scare me. How about we get to that shopping instead?"

They spent the next hour wandering up Cottonwood Street and down Pinion checking out the vendor booths. Lori bought a necklace for her mother from a jewelry vendor and a sterling silver dog charm for her mentor, Nic Callahan, Eternity Springs' veterinarian. Molly bought some scented lotion to give as a thank-you gift to Lori's mom, Sarah, while Mason loitered in the booth where a vendor sold classic comic books. At the VISTAS ART GALLERY booth, Mason gestured toward a display of wood carvings. "That eagle looks almost real."

"Our friend Sage represents some wonderful artists," Lori said. "And she's super-talented herself. Let's go inside the gallery. I want to show you a sculpture on display."

Ten minutes later, Mason whipped out his credit card and finished his Christmas shopping by purchasing a painting by a Colorado artist for his parents. Molly watched his excitement over having found the perfect gift, and again, her spirits took a dip.

She had to buy separate Christmas gifts for her separated parents. She had to make separate phone calls about her engagement. She'd have to make a trip to West Texas and one to New York to show off her new bling. She hated this!

Stop it, she silently chided herself as she left Vistas with Mason and Lori. *Deal with it. Don't let them steal your joy. Not today.* Doing so was silly. It wasn't like Mom and Dad separated yesterday. They'd been apart for years now. She should be used to it.

She'd never be used to it.

As the town's church bells pealed five o'clock, Molly lifted her face toward the sunny sky and soaked in the warmth. She recognized that she was being oversensitive about the whole parent thing today. Still, since she'd watched Lori joking around with her mother the night before, unsettling emotions had churned in Molly's heart.

She spied the Angel's Rest booth up ahead and, ready for a distraction, focused on it like a lifeline. Celeste had three large plastic storage boxes lying open with stacks of plastic Bubble Wrap and tissue paper ready for use. She was dressed in denim Capri pants, a gold polo shirt sporting the Angel's Rest logo, and white sneakers. Her sun visor had angels' wings embroidered across the headband. Though she was old enough to be Lori's grandmother, Celeste was one of the most extraordinary women that Molly had ever met.

Also, she discovered Celeste had a heavenly voice as the older woman segued from singing "Hark the Herald Angels Sing" to "Angels We Have Heard on High." Then, noting the college students' arrival, Celeste winked and altered the lyrics. "Sweetly singing to all the tourists."

In the booth next to Celeste's representing the Reese family business, The Trading Post grocery store, Sarah Reese stacked her home-baked gingerbread men into a cookie tin. Lori's mom chimed in with a slightly out-of-tune version of a song from the Rudolph Christmas cartoon. "Who brings in the silver and gold, silver and gold, so that I can pay my insurance at the end of the month."

"Joy to the World," Celeste trilled.

"Y'all are so lame," Lori teased, swiping a cookie from her mother's tin. "Loveable, but lame."

Sarah slapped her daughter's hand. "Brat."

"Sorry we're late, Ms. Blessing," Mason said to Celeste. "I stopped to buy my parents' Christmas gift at the gallery booth up the street."

"Not a problem. I had shoppers here until just a minute ago. Three lovely ladies from Tennessee bought six angel figurines, three angel ornaments, two angel tree toppers, and an angel-themed Christmas tree skirt."

"I thought they might buy everything you had left, Celeste," Sarah said, offering cookies to Mason and Molly. "You don't have much to pack up as it is."

"Nor do you," Celeste replied, beaming. "I think we can officially declare our *Christmas in August* event a success. I really think you should consider opening a bakery here in town."

"There go the waistlines of Eternity Springs," Lori quipped as she, Mason, and Molly set down their purchases and got to work.

In addition to the items offered for sale, each vendor booth included signs, display racks, and tables. Celeste turned Mason loose with a screwdriver to disassemble items in both the Angel's Rest booth and that of the Trading Post. Lori and Molly were tasked with wrapping fragile items in pieces of packaging film and storing them in plastic tubs. While they worked, the conversation turned to previous town festivals. Lori and her mother shared a story of a baking disaster during Lori's childhood.

The mother-daughter banter turned Molly's thoughts toward her own mother. Once upon a time, she and her mom shared a similarly easy and affectionate relationship. Now, not so much. The days of laughing together while Mom attempted to teach Molly Fumble-finger how to knit, for instance, were long gone. She picked up an angel figurine and carefully wrapped it in Bubble Wrap.

"Molly, dear, what's wrong?" Celeste asked a few minutes later.

"You're crying," Sarah observed, her tone concerned.

I am? Well, perfect.

Mason winced. "Aw, Molly."

"Nothing's wrong," Molly said, swiping her cheeks

with the back of her hand. She set the figurine carefully into a storage tub and added, "I'm emotional. Mason and I just got engaged."

Even as she blinked back fresh moisture, she held up her left hand, wiggled her fingers, and tried her best to smile. The diamond flashed in the sunlight. Sarah moved forward to wrap her arms around Molly and said, "Congratulations."

"Thank you."

Celeste beamed at Mason. "That's a beautiful engagement ring, Mason."

"Thanks," Mason said. "Picking it out was tougher than my organic chemistry and quantum mechanics classes put together."

"Just thinking about classes like that makes my head hurt," Sarah said, her tone light though she gazed at Molly with concern.

Celeste pulled a packet of tissues from beneath one of her display tables. She offered it to Molly. "So, dear, these are tears of happiness?"

"Yes. No. I don't know." Molly wiped the tears from her cheeks and blew her nose. "It's complicated."

Celeste clicked her tongue and glanced from Molly to Mason and back to Molly again. "I don't want to intrude, but is there anything we can do to help?"

"I wish you could help. It's the wedding. It's my parents." Molly met Sarah's gaze and added, "It's the wedding *and* my parents."

"They don't approve of your choice?" Nic asked.

"No, that's not it. They love Mason."

"Your mom loves me," Mason corrected. "Your dad tolerates me. He doesn't think any guy is good enough for you."

Sarah nodded. "Typical attitude from a father. So, what's the problem?"

Molly tugged a second tissue from the pack, then swiped new tears off her cheeks. "My parents don't speak to each other. They haven't seen each other in over three years."

"Oh, no," Celeste said.

Sarah frowned. "I know your mother is a renowned concert pianist who travels the world, but I didn't realize your parents were divorced."

"They're not divorced," Mason clarified.

"They just hate each other," Molly added. "And I hate even thinking about it."

That pretty much stopped the questions, and they worked the next few minutes in silence. Lori's mom loaded the last of her leftover baked goods into her nearby truck, then pitched in the help Lori wrap glass Christmas ornaments.

Mason slipped a knitted angel puppet onto his hand and used it to "kiss" Molly's cheek. "You okay?"

"Yes." Molly gave him a watery smile. "I'm so happy, Mason. Just feeling a little overwhelmed. Thinking about our marriage makes me think about my parents' marriage, and that blues my mood. Which is stupid. I should be able to just be happy."

"I don't think it's stupid at all." Celeste reached over

and patted Molly's hand. "Nothing gives us quite as much joy or causes quite as much pain as family."

"Is your mother's career the problem?" Sarah asked. "Your father is a rancher, right?"

Molly fingered a glass ornament shaped like an angel's wings. "Commercial farmer and rancher, yes. He's tied to the land, but Mom's career was something they seemed to manage okay. Then four years ago . . ."

She closed her eyes and shuddered. Mason gave her shoulders a comforting squeeze. "Her uncle committed suicide."

"Oh, I'm so sorry," Celeste said.

"He was Mom's brother and my dad's best friend and business partner."

Sarah shook her head, her violet-blue eyes soft with sympathy. "What a tragedy for your family, Molly."

Molly's throat worked. "Nothing has been the same since."

Mason took her hand and brought it to his mouth for a comforting kiss.

She gave him a grateful smile, then added, "My parents are masterful when it comes to avoiding one another. I've tried everything to get them together. Conference calls, 'accidental' meetings—nothing works. It takes a miracle to get him to leave the ranch, and she won't even take a flight that crosses West Texas airspace. They've already figured out a way for them to attend graduation in December without interaction."

"Oh, Molly." Celeste clicked her tongue. "Are you

afraid that they won't attend the wedding? Or maybe attend and cause a scene?"

"No." She picked up a red heart-shaped glass ornament and cradled it in her hand. "I know they love me, and I have faith they'll be civil to one another on my special day. I even think they'll try to get along. But honestly, what I really want is for the tension to be dealt with beforehand so that I'm not on pins and needles all the time."

"They put you in the middle?" Sarah asked.

"Yes. Not on purpose, though. They don't mean to do it, but it happens, and somehow that makes it worse. If I go to the ranch instead of going to New York, she's hurt. If I see her instead of him, he goes quiet. It's a silent tug-of-war, and I want it to stop, at least on my wedding day. I want to think about our marriage that day, not the disaster of my parents' marriage."

"I see." Her arms crossed, Celeste lifted one hand to thoughtfully tap her lips with her index finger.

Sarah said, "I don't know your mother, but I've spoken with your dad on the phone, Molly. He strikes me as a reasonable person. You should say to him what you've just said to us. I'll bet he'll listen and do what he can to make it right for you."

"Maybe," Molly said glumly.

Celeste asked, "Do you have a date for the wedding in mind yet?"

The couple glanced at each other, then Molly said, "We briefly discussed it earlier. But, first, we'll need to speak with our families and get everyone to check their calendars."

"I'm hoping for shortly after graduation," Mason said. "I wouldn't want to start a new job and then ask off for a honeymoon."

Lori suggested, "You should have a Christmas wedding. Maybe on the weekend between Christmas and New Year's."

"And where will it take place?"

Molly winced and bit her bottom lip. "I don't know. I split my time between Dad's ranch in Texas and Mom's place in New York."

"Knowing them, they'll want us to do two weddings," Mason drawled.

"Nonsense." Celeste dismissed that with a wave. "You two should get married on neutral ground. Have a destination wedding."

"You mean like Hawaii?" Mason rubbed the back of his neck. "I don't know, Ms. Blessing. That would probably be okay with my parents. They like to travel every chance they get. But we'd also like to have our friends at our wedding. Our friends are mostly poor college kids, so asking them to make a big trip really doesn't work."

"And I don't want to ask my parents to pay for something like that," Molly added. "Money is tight for Dad, and he's too proud to let Mom pay for everything. So, it's better for everyone if we keep this wedding low-key."

"Actually, I was thinking of someplace much closer

and more economical than Hawaii," Celeste said. "Why don't you get married here in Eternity Springs? It's within driving distance from Texas, so travel doesn't need to be too expensive. You'd have a historic church for the ceremony, and Angel's Rest is a lovely venue for a reception. I happen to know that your friends could get an extra-special deal on their rooms. Our college student winter discount is even better than what we offer in summer."

Interest lit both Mason's and Molly's eyes as they glanced at one another. "In a town this small," Sarah said, "your parents couldn't avoid each other for long."

"That's a thought," Molly said.

Celeste added, "I know of a perfect place for a secluded honeymoon if you want to stay in the area. Sarah, you've seen what the Timberlakes have done to Bear's yurt, have you not?"

"Yurt?" Mason asked.

"It's a year-round universal recreation tent."

"You want me to spend my honeymoon in a tent!" Molly exclaimed.

Sarah laughed. "That yurt is no ordinary tent. It was luxurious before our friends bought it, but after their upgrades, it could compete with a five-star hotel. It's their romantic getaway, but I'm sure they'd let you use it."

Lori nodded decisively. "You should totally do it."

"It does sound awesome," Mason said.

"You and your parents could come here for Christmas," Celeste said. "You'll have last-minute preparations to make. That way, you could deal with the tension before your wedding day."

Mason nodded. "I'll bet my family would come here for Christmas, too. We could spend the holidays together and put off the whole 'Whose family do we spend Christmas with?' decision for another year."

"That would be awesome." Molly took a long look around, her lips pursed in thought. "Lori says it's beautiful here at Christmastime. Cold, but beautiful."

A wicked glint entered Mason's eyes as he added, "Good snuggling weather."

"I'd be honored to bake your wedding cake," Sarah offered. "Ali Timberlake could do the catering, too. She's a wonderful cook."

Molly met Mason's gaze with a questioning look.

"It could be great," he said.

"Or a disaster," she replied.

"Either way, it'd break the ice with your parents before the wedding." He shrugged and added, "It's up to you, Molly. You're the bride, and I'm fine with whatever you want."

"I'm the bride," she repeated, a smile slowly spreading across her face. "How cool is that?"

"Totally cool," her Maid of Honor agreed.

Molly considered the question for another minute, then nodded. "Okay, let's do it. Unless our families have an objection that we haven't anticipated, let's get married here in Eternity Springs at Christmas."

"Excellent." Celeste stepped forward and gave them

both a hug. "When we finish here, let's stop by the office and get it on the calendar. How exciting."

"A winter wedding in Eternity Springs!" Celeste exclaimed.

Mason leaned over and kissed Molly lightly on the mouth. "And with any luck, a family Merry Christmas at Angel's Rest."

"Merry Christmas? With my parents?" Molly closed her eyes and grimaced. "I hope it doesn't turn into *Gunfight at the O.K. Corral*."

Celeste laughed and gave Molly another hug. "Don't worry, child. I have a feeling this will be a Christmas season of joy for the Stapleton family."

"From your mouth to God's ears, Celeste."

"That's the way it works, dear. That's the way it works."

London

Emma Stapleton logged off the online telephone call with a trembling hand, then stood staring at the screen, lost in thought, blinking back tears. Her manager, Nicco Berlini, walked into their suite at the Savoy and halted abruptly. *"Cara mia,"* he said, worry in his tone. "You are as pale as a ghost. What is wrong? What terrible thing has happened?"

"Not a terrible thing," she replied, proud that her voice didn't shake. "A good thing. A wonderful thing."

When she didn't continue, Nicco crossed the room to her, took her hands, and lifted them to his lips for a kiss. "And what wonderful thing puts such sorrow in those big blue eyes?"

"It's not sorrow," she insisted. "It's not. Truly. I'm happy."

Nicco arched his brows.

"My Molly is getting married."

"Aha," he murmured, his gaze full of caring and concern.

Emma's mouth lifted in a crooked smile. When the man looked at her like that, she could almost forget that he could give Lothario a run for his money. Nicco was a cliché: tall, dark, and handsome. His thick, black-as-midnight hair set off liquid brown eyes that smoldered on a whim. His nose was a thin Roman blade, his cheekbones sharp, his lips thickly sensuous. He dressed in Armani and flirted with anything in a skirt. Emma trusted him with her career and money, but her heart was strictly off-limits.

Been there, done that, with a too-handsome-for-her-own-good man.

Not that Jared had been a horndog like Nicco. No, his sins against her were something else entirely.

"So young Mason popped the question, did he?" Nicco asked, his voice gentle. "You told me you adore the young man. Why the watery eyes?"

Emma opened her mouth, then couldn't find the words. How could she verbalize the emotions running through her when they didn't make sense? She *did* adore

Mason. She *was* happy for Molly. So why did the thought of being the mother of the bride make her want to cry?

Two words: Jared Stapleton.

This should be the moment when the bride's mother turned to the bride's father and said, "Our baby is all grown up."

Instead, she was on one side of the Atlantic sharing a hotel suite with an Italian stallion, and he was undoubtedly on the other, holed up on that godforsaken ranch with his . . . cows. How sad was that?

"Where did the years go, Nicco? When did I get to be old enough to have a son-in-law?"

"It's your own fault, *bella*. You should not have let that cowboy seduce you when you were twelve."

She laughed then, as he'd surely known she would.

"Now, come love. Dry your eyes and take me to dinner. We should have Prosecco, I think, to celebrate. Then, tomorrow you can begin your diet."

"My diet!"

He shrugged. "You are a beautiful woman, a young Sophia Loren. But I suspect that if you were to climb upon the scale tonight, my Emma, you would discover that you have gained as much as three pounds in the past month. That might be acceptable for a concert pianist, but as a mother of the bride? Impossible!"

"I hate you, Nicco."

"You adore me, Emma, love. And I want you to know that I will overlook the thickness in your waist if you'll finally abandon the silly nonsense about being a married woman and take me to your bed."

Drily, she replied, "How kind of you."

"What can I say? I am a prince."

"My waist isn't thick."

He shrugged. "You are not twenty-five anymore, and three pounds can easily become thirteen. I will not cater to your vanity, my love. That is why you hired me, no?"

Initially, she'd hired him with the idea of driving Jared crazy, but in the past two years, he'd become a dear friend and an indispensable manager. But, of course, she dared not say that too often, so instead, she grumbled, "I don't know why I haven't fired you."

"Because I refuse to accept anything less than your best, and this is not an easy job. What has happened to your self-discipline of late? I shudder to think what might become of you were I not here to keep you in check."

Emma had the sudden urge to stick out her tongue at the man. Instead, she reached defiantly for the candy dish and one of the Parisian chocolate-covered caramels she kept in constant supply.

Nicco grinned as she gleefully unwrapped the candy. "Ah, but I do so love that fire in your eyes. So, indulge tonight, love, for tomorrow we begin preparations for the Milan performance and your meeting with the devil himself."

The chocolate halfway to her mouth, Emma froze. "Jared."

Nicco folded his arms. "This is why you need me, Emma. You had not put those particular pieces together, no? As the mother of the bride, you will not be able to avoid the father of the bride. Nor he you."

He was right. As usual, Nicco was right. "Despite everything else, he's been a good father to Molly. We can't let our . . . disagreements . . . ruin the day for Molly."

"No, you can't."

Emma turned her head toward the full-length mirror on the far wall of the luxurious suite. *Jared. Not three pounds. Eight.* She'd gained eight pounds in the three years since she'd last seen Jared. Eleven pounds since they'd married twenty-three years ago. "Their wedding date is December twenty-eighth. How many weeks until then?"

He considered the question. "Seventeen."

She tossed the chocolate into the nearest trash can. "I want to make him choke on his alfalfa."

"*Brava!* Now, let's head to the gym."

West Texas

The ringtone on Jared Stapleton's phone played Jimmy Buffet's "Little Miss Magic" just as he completed one last futures trade for the day. He smiled with pleasure as he abandoned his computer mouse, reached for his phone, and connected the FaceTime call. "Sunshine. This is a nice surprise."

"Hi, Daddy," Molly said.

"How are things in Colorado? Are you enjoying your vacation?"

"I am."

Jared drank in the sight of his daughter as she gave him a rundown of her past few days' activities. Molly looked happy, which made *him* happy—until she got to the reason for the call. His baby was engaged to be married. He tried to be positive. God's honest truth, he did try. But when they'd ended the call ten minutes later, he couldn't deny the ache in his heart.

His little girl was all grown up.

And her mother wasn't here to share the melancholy with him.

"Dammit, Emma," he muttered.

He remembered the day Molly had been born. She'd been an "oops" baby, conceived after he and Emma were married but before she'd finished school. He'd just finished his shift waiting tables at a local restaurant when the call came that Emma was in labor. He'd rushed home, they'd hurried to the hospital, and fifteen stress-filled hours later, Emma delivered Mary Elizabeth.

His baby girl had owned his heart from her very first breath.

Those early years hadn't been easy. Jared had been at UConn on a basketball scholarship when his friend and teammate Frank Rossi introduced him to his knockout of a sister. They dated for the next two years. After Jared's graduation, they'd married, and he'd moved to Boston, where he worked two jobs to support his little family while Emma finished school. A Berklee College of Music student, she had taught piano lessons in her spare time, of which there was hardly any. But they'd made it, and the shared struggle had made them stronger, he'd always thought. Looking back, they'd been the best days of his life.

A knock at his ranch house office door shook him from his reverie, and his sister, Shelby Montrose, stuck her head in the room and asked, "Got a minute, Jared?"

"Sure. Come on in," he replied, glad for the distraction.

Shelby was tall and lanky, with dark hair and a complexion tanned from the summertime sun. Three years younger than Jared and a numbers geek, Shelby had dived into the muck alongside him four years ago and started shoveling. Together, they'd brought Wildcatter Farms and Ranch back from the brink of bankruptcy. She'd done a fine job as their chief financial officer. Jared was grateful that she'd agreed to move back to the Wildcatter to work after Emma's brother, Frank, almost destroyed them.

She carried a manila file folder and looked worried as she sat across from him. Jared didn't like that look. "What's wrong?"

She flipped her long, wavy hair behind her shoulder. "I've been running the numbers. I'm afraid we'll have to go back to the bank, Jared."

His stomach sank, and he grimaced. He'd been afraid of this for weeks now.

Damned if he'd go down that road—not again. They hadn't scraped and scrapped and scrambled their way back from the brink of losing the ranch to put it back in jeopardy again now.

They spent twenty minutes discussing their financial issues, and then Shelby tossed out her verbal grenade. "I just don't see another way around it, Jared, unless . . . we still have an offer on the table for the Johnston farm."

"I'm not selling any more land."

"Then you'll be borrowing from the bank," she fired back. "Even with the rise in beef prices and a strong alfalfa crop, we're still looking at red ink come the end of the fiscal year."

"I have some money set aside that I can tap." He named a figure, then added, "It's not a lot, but maybe we could scrape by."

"You're not sinking your savings into the Wildcatter, Jared. Not again. Mom and I have already discussed it. You've done enough."

Exactly. He'd almost lost the family ranch. "It's my fault that our financial—"

"Stop it! That was four years ago now, Jared. It's over. Done. That particular excuse has run its course."

Jared set his jaw. If he lived to be one hundred, it wouldn't be over. It wouldn't be done.

Shelby plowed on. "You hired me to do a job around here, Jared. You need to let me do it. I recommend you sell that farm and the mineral rights that go with it. We still have fifteen hundred acres at the Wildcatter. We don't need those three hundred and—"

"Molly called a few minutes ago," he interjected, hoping to change the direction of the conversation.

Shelby hesitated, tilted her head, and studied him. With a knowing note to her tone that signaled her awareness of his ploy, she asked, "And what did the squirt have to say?"

"She's getting married."

Shelby sat up straight and smiled with delight. "Go, Mason! I was a little worried when her birthday came and went without a ring. Better late than never, though, right?"

Jared tried to smile, but it must have been a sickly one because his sister's expression dimmed. "Oh, Jared. Don't tell me you have something against Mason."

"No, not really. He's a good guy."

"I know that Molly loves him very much."

"Yeah," he agreed glumly.

Shelby offered a sympathetic smile. "Feeling a little daddy sad, are you?"

"I guess so. Seems like just yesterday, Molly was riding her scooter on the driveway and turning cart-wheels across the backyard. I'll never forget the time she and Emma—" He broke off abruptly and snapped his jaw shut.

Emma. That's twice in an hour that he'd spoken her name aloud. Bet he hadn't done that in a year.

Shelby didn't mention his slip, but the look in her

eyes revealed that she'd noticed. "Have they set a date yet?"

"December twenty-eighth. She told me she wants a destination wedding in Lori Reese's hometown." It saddened him that she wouldn't get married here, but he wasn't surprised. He doubted her mother would return to the Wildcatter, even for their daughter's wedding.

"Eternity Springs," Shelby said, nodding. "Lori showed me pictures of it when I visited Molly in College Station last spring. It looks like a charming little place." She hesitated, then asked, "You will go to the wedding, won't you?"

"Of course, I'll go to the wedding!" Jared scowled at his sister. "I'll pay for it, too. I am her father."

"One more reason you need to keep that nest egg available. Weddings are expensive." Shelby studied her fingernails. "And I assume her mother will be there."

Jared couldn't sit still any longer. He pushed to his feet and paced to the bar, where he poured himself a scotch. "Do you want something to drink?"

Shelby sighed as she rose from her seat and gathered her papers. She crossed the room to her brother, went up on her tiptoes, and kissed him on the cheek. "I love you, Jared. You are a great brother and a wonderful father. Before Frank screwed it up, you and Emma were more in love than any two people I've ever met. I know that what happened was horrible for you both. I know that each of you has a right to be angry. But hasn't the silence gone on long enough? It's time you and Emma talked. Molly's wedding can give you that opportunity."

"I love you, too, Shelby," he replied.

She waited, but when he didn't address the rest of her comments, she sighed and left his office. Once alone, Jared finished his drink and exited the ranch house. The night was dark, and the sky had a million stars. He looked above into the starlit heavens and wondered where in the world his wife was tonight.

Did he even care?

PART II

December 21
Eternity Springs, Colorado

Emma Stapleton clutched the wheel of her rental SUV with a white-knuckled grip as she drove over the summit of Sinner's Prayer Pass. Although the snow was piled high on either side of the road, the plow had been out, and the road was dry. She had experience driving in the mountains in winter, so the drive itself wasn't the reason for her nervousness. She didn't fear sliding off the hill and crashing to her death. Instead, what scared Emma was the knowledge of what awaited her arrival in the town nestled in the valley below.

A family reunion. A family Christmas. A family wedding.

It promised to be a week from hell.

"At least I look good," she murmured to her traveling companion, a three-month-old mixed-breed puppy. The poor little guy had been abandoned by his owners in the suite next to hers at the Hotel Imperial in Vienna. Emma's frequent travel made it silly for her to own a dog, but after listening to his pitiful whines and the hotel staff's tales of animal shelter overcrowding, she couldn't turn her back on the pup. So, she'd named him Mozart and allowed him to sleep at the foot of her bed.

She awoke every morning to find him snuggled against her.

Now, Mozart lay snoozing in his pet carrier, so he didn't respond to her observation. That didn't prevent her from continuing the conversation.

"New hairstyle, new makeup, new clothes—two sizes smaller, thank you very much. I have muscle definition in my arms and a spring in my step because I am confident. I am bursting with self-confidence." As she headed down the mountain, she broke into song, channeling her inner Julie Andrews playing Maria on the way to meet Captain von Trapp by singing "I Have Confidence." She sang with as much heart as she could manage—considering that her heart was all but in her throat.

Was Jared already at Angel's Rest? They'd managed graduation without setting eyes on each other. Would he see her when she arrived? Would he come out to meet her car? Or would he wait for her to approach him? Was she getting to Eternity Springs ahead of him? If so, would she see him when he arrived? Would she go out to meet his car? Would she wait for him to approach her?

"Besides which, you see, I—" Emma quit singing as her SUV negotiated the final switchback before the road leveled out and led into Eternity Springs. She croaked out, "I am confidently scared to death."

Her GPS guided her down what appeared to be the main street in town. She had to admit Molly's description of "charming" was spot-on. Eternity Springs was a scene right off a Christmas card. Snowdrifts hugged the base of Victorian storefronts bedecked with evergreen garlands and wreaths sporting bright red ribbons. Potted fir trees stood beside entry doors trimmed in decorations in keeping with the business conducted within. Toothbrushes and dental floss decorated the tree in front of a dental office. The library's tree was hung with dozens of miniature books. The tree at a barbershop was wrapped in red and white ribbon and plastic combs in red and green. Emma couldn't help but smile despite her nervousness.

At the intersection of Spruce and Fifth, her GPS instructed her to turn right to reach her destination, Angel's Rest Healing Center and Spa. But when she spied a church steeple and the sign for St. Stephen's off to the left, she went in that direction. Molly and Mason were to be married in this church next week. "Oh, it's lovely," she murmured to her dog when she got her first good look at the small wooden structure.

It was another greeting card view—a white wooden

church with a black shingled roof and steeple, evergreen wreaths sporting big red bows on the doors, and a manger scene in the yard. Picture-perfect. Molly had chosen a wonderful venue for the wedding. But, as happened so often lately, when Emma thought about her little girl getting married, her throat tightened, and she blinked back tears.

"I hope I make it through this, Mozart," she said, then she circled the block and continued up Fifth toward a quaint wooden bridge that spanned a frozen creek. Beyond it stood a beautifully carved wooden sign that read ANGEL'S REST.

Angel's Rest Healing Center and Spa was a large estate with numerous structures, including landscaped hot-spring pools whose steaming surfaces looked warm and inviting. The estate's centerpiece was a multistory Victorian mansion that sat proudly at the mountain's base. Cavanaugh House, Emma knew, since it was listed on the wedding invitation. *What a grand old mansion.*

She pulled her car around the circular drive and parked beneath the Porte-cochere. Switching off her engine, she took a deep, bracing breath, picked up her purse and Mozart's carrier, and opened the door.

The cold mountain air smelled like Christmas.

The door opened, and an older woman wearing red velvet trimmed in white fur stood smiling and waving and saying, "Welcome to Angel's Rest."

Never mind Julie Andrews and *The Sound of Music*. This was Rosemary Clooney in *White Christmas*—just a little older. "What a great dress," Emma said as she stepped inside.

"Thank you." The lovely woman beamed like lights on a Christmas tree. "Tonight is the holiday party for our quilting group, the Patchwork Angels. Attending in costume just puts me right in the party spirit. I'm Celeste Blessing, and you must be dear Molly's mother."

"Yes. I'm Emma Stapleton."

"If you'll allow me to briefly go fangirl, I saw you perform at Carnegie Hall three years ago. I must say that your interpretation of Tchaikovsky brought tears to my eyes."

"Thank you." Emma smiled at the compliment, then glanced cautiously around. When she didn't see Jared, she relaxed a little bit.

"Molly and Mason have gone snowmobiling with some other young people in town. She told me your husband is due to arrive around five. She's reserved our private parlor for a family meal at seven. We'll be serving tasting portions of the menu you have chosen for the reception. Is that acceptable to you?"

"That will be wonderful." It was almost four now. That gave her three hours. Emma felt as if she'd just been awarded a temporary stay of execution, and the fact that she felt that way annoyed her. It was high time she and Jared found a way to interact. This avoidance campaign they'd engaged in for so long was childish.

She was shown to a lovely feminine room decorated

in cabbage roses and antique furniture, including a graceful wooden rocker that sat before a fireplace furnished with electric logs. A quilt done in shades of ivory and white lay draped across the chair's back. She tipped the teenage boy who brought up her luggage, then unpacked and surrendered to the lure of the rocker with Mozart snoozing happily in her lap.

Emma slept and dreamed of being lost in a field of alfalfa.

For the fifth time in as many minutes, Jared second-guessed his decision to wear a suit to this family dinner. Molly would likely show up in jeans, and Emma . . . well . . . the old Emma would have worn a dress, but he didn't have a clue what this Emma would do. Better to be overdressed than underdressed, right? This was no different than a meeting with bankers. Best not to give the opposition the upper hand in any area.

Staring at his reflection in the freestanding full-length mirror, he didn't see a six-foot-four rancher with green eyes and brown hair going gray at the temples. He saw a grim-faced man wearing the tie his daughter had given him last Christmas who needed to stop tugging at his collar and badly wanted a scotch.

The fact that he was tense about tonight annoyed him.

The fact that he looked forward to seeing Emma again worried him.

Their marriage was over. Done. Finished.

She traveled the world with an Italian gigolo—her "manager." Jared would be hanged if he'd forgive her of that.

Not that she'd ever shown any inclination to forgive him.

Jared wasn't without blame for their trouble. He shared responsibility for what happened, and he'd never once tried to deny that. He'd spent the past few years trying to atone and live with it. Trying to live with *himself*—with the ugly words that Emma had shouted at him that terrible night playing through his mind in an unending loop.

It's your fault, Jared. None of this would have happened if you hadn't introduced Frank to horse racing or if you'd paid attention to the books. You and those stupid breeders, those stupid horses.

Grimly, Jared gave his tie one last straightening nudge, then turned away from the mirror and checked the mantel clock. Five till seven. It was time.

He exited his room and made his way downstairs. The parlor door was closed, with a sign that read PRIVATE PARTY hanging from a clip on the door frame. He drew a deep breath, knocked, then opened the door.

Molly stood beside the fireplace, where a real fire burned, and upon seeing her, his breath caught. *She's all grown up, the image of her mother at that age.*

Molly wore a classic black sheath dress and the family heirloom pearls he'd given her for college graduation. The natural red highlights in her dark auburn hair glistened in the firelight, and her expression beamed with pleasure when she saw him. "Daddy!"

She was across the room and in his arms in a heartbeat. Jared closed his eyes and enjoyed the experience, missing those years when this was a daily occurrence. "Hello, beautiful."

"I'm so glad you're here. I had nightmares that a blizzard of epic proportions would descend on the valley, and the authorities would close the mountain pass, and you wouldn't be able to get to Eternity Springs."

"I wouldn't have let a blizzard stop me." As she stepped back, he stared down into her face and shook his head. "Mason better know just what a treasure he's getting."

"I'm the one who is getting the treasure, Dad. Mason treats me like a queen."

From the corner of his eye, Jared saw movement in the doorway. He turned his head and absorbed the blow. Emma.

Now there was a queen. She looked gorgeous. Regal. Sophisticated. Unreachable. She, too, wore a black dress and pearls, and he couldn't help but wonder if they were the pearls he'd given her years ago or a new string. Had she replaced his pearls like she'd replaced him?

"Mom!" Repeating her earlier welcome gesture, Molly took three steps toward her mother, then abruptly stopped. "Oh, look. I don't believe this. We're wearing the same dress."

Emma's gaze breezed over their daughter, then she smiled. "So, am I dressing too young for my age, or are you dressing too old?"

Jared gave no conscious thought to the words that emerged from his mouth. "The dress is perfect for you both."

Emma's gaze met his. Her smile went brittle. "Hello, Jared."

His reply was just as stiff. "Hello, Emma."

Molly made a little snort of disgust, then hugged her mother. "I was just telling Dad that I've been having nightmares about a blizzard that kept everyone from reaching Eternity Springs."

Jared could understand why blizzards had been on his daughter's mind. After all, it felt as if the snowstorm of the century had just swept into the room with his wife.

Molly continued, "But you're here, and Dad's here, and Mason arrived with his parents earlier today, so I have the people I need the most. I'm going to quit worrying about blizzards."

Molly could quit worrying about blizzards, but Jared was afraid he might lose a toe or two to frostbite.

Emma looked around the room, then her gaze settled on the table set for three. "Mason isn't joining us?"

"No. I wanted tonight to be just the three of us." She took a bracing breath, then said, "I think it's time for some candid conversation, don't you?"

Again, Jared's and Emma's gazes met. She looked just about as happy at the idea as he felt. Jared spied the bar in the corner of the room and decided that a scotch was definitely in order. "Can I get either of you something to drink?"

"No, thanks," Molly said. "I'll have wine with dinner."

"I'll have a scotch, please," Emma said.

She'd surprised him yet again. When had she started drinking scotch? "Ice?"

"No, thank you."

Okay, then. He fixed the drinks, pouring himself a double, as Molly continued: "I've put quite a bit of thought into how I'd like this dinner of ours to progress. But first, I want to thank you both for agreeing to spend Christmas with me here before the wedding. I know you would rather be just about anywhere else, with anybody else, but you are doing this for me. I recognize it and appreciate it more than I can say."

Jared handed Emma her drink. Their fingers brushed, and they both jerked, sending the liquor sloshing up the sides of the crystal lowball glass. They didn't speak. He felt like he had a mountain sitting on his chest.

Emma said, "Molly, I'm sure your father and I want your wedding to be all you've dreamed of. So, if spending Christmas together helps accomplish that, then everything's fine."

Molly's sad eyes and shaky little smile spoke volumes. Jared felt the sting of guilt he'd grown accustomed to experiencing whenever he thought about the effect of his and Emma's estrangement on their only child.

"Good," his daughter said in response to her mother's comment. "I've been hoping you feel that way because, with that in mind, I have a special request. Consider it my Christmas gift or my wedding gift. I don't really care which. I want you to know that I want this more than anything else you could give me."

Jared's stomach sank. Surely, she wouldn't ask for some sort of reconciliation as a gift. She had to know that wouldn't be reasonable. If she were three or thirteen, he could see that she might ask for the impossible, but at twenty-three? She should know better.

Although . . . Jared stole another glance at Emma. *Was* it impossible? Was there any chance that Emma would seize upon the excuse and say, "Let's give it a try"? What would he do if she did?

Her body language gave no clue as to what she was thinking. His heartbeat accelerated. He licked his suddenly dry lips. With her voice calm and quiet, Emma asked, "What is it that you want, Molly?"

Molly laced her fingers, straightened her spine, and met her mother's gaze, then her father's. Once she had their total attention, she said, "Mom. Dad. As a gift to me, I'd like you two to get a divorce."

Jared closed his eyes.

❄

Emma's heart twisted in pain. *A divorce?* Molly wanted them to get a divorce?

Emma sliced a look toward Jared. Had this been his idea? Had he put their daughter up to making this request? She couldn't tell by looking at him, which only intensified the hurt. Once upon a time, she could read him like a book.

Molly continued, "I know this might seem like a strange request, but I've thought a lot about it. It's obvious your marriage is over. Neither of you is happy. Neither of you is moving on with your life. That's no way to live."

As she spoke, she looked from Emma to Jared, then back to Emma again. "If you've been waiting for me to grow up or graduate, you don't have to wait any longer. You don't have to worry about me any longer. But as long as you two are stuck in this . . . limbo . . . I worry about you. I've been worried about you both for years now, and I think it's time to stop. Don't you? Please, just go ahead and get a divorce. I know you'll both be happier."

Emma couldn't believe what she was hearing. She didn't know what to say or how to react. This suggestion had come entirely out of the blue. She waited, hoping Jared would speak first.

His mouth remained stubbornly closed.

Figures. She cleared her throat. "Molly, I—"

A knock at the door interrupted her, and the door swung open. Celeste glided inside, followed by an attractive blond woman who was Emma's age or maybe a little older. They both carried trays loaded with food. "I hope you are hungry," Celeste said. "Jared and Emma Stapleton, I'd like you to meet Ali Timberlake, owner of the Yellow Kitchen, the best restaurant in Colorado."

"Oh, Celeste," the other woman said with a roll of her blue eyes as she set her tray on the buffet.

Emma was thrilled at the interruption. She and Ali Timberlake had spoken on the phone several times as they planned the reception menu. She stepped forward, her hand outstretched as she said, "Ali, it's lovely to finally meet you. I'm Emma."

"And I'm Jared," he said, coming up behind Emma.

Ali shook their hands, complimented Emma on her talent, then presented the items on the buffet. "If anything doesn't suit your fancy or if you want to add something to the menu, just let me know. We still have time to make changes."

"I'm sure we're going to love everything, Mrs. Timberlake," Molly said. "Mason still goes into moans of rapture about your Alfredo sauce any time Italian food gets mentioned."

Emma asked a few reception-menu questions, more as a delaying tactic than out of curiosity, but soon the other women left the Stapleton family alone. Emma and Jared stood frozen in place. Molly spoke with false brightness. "We'd better eat while it's hot."

Emma had sat through uncomfortable meals in the past, but this one topped them all. The food was delicious, and Emma had no concerns about that part of the wedding. Molly babbled on about centerpieces and music, and Emma's discomfort grew. This was ridiculous. They were acting like children. She was just about to speak when Jared set down his fork and said, "Enough. This is absurd. Molly, please excuse yourself and allow your mother and me some privacy."

Molly glanced from one parent to the other and hesitated. "I'm not sure—"

"Molly," Emma snapped. "This is what you wanted when you set this little meeting up. Let us deal with it."

Their daughter could be as stubborn as Rocky Mountain granite. "But I haven't eaten my dinner."

"Load your plate on the way out," Jared said.

She huffed, lifted her nose, gave her hair a dramatic toss, and finally sashayed out of the room. When the door shut behind her—loudly—an unexpected thing happened.

Emma's gaze met Jared's . . . and they shared a smile.

For Emma, it was a flashback to another time, a good time when their family was . . . a family. The smile was a pin that popped the balloon of tension hanging in the room, but as that force dissipated, another emotion filled the void. Sadness. She felt it, and she could see it on Jared's face.

How had they come to this?

The ugliness of their fight in the wake of Frank's suicide had been the catalyst, of course. They both had been mired in pain and guilt and furious at the actions the other had taken. They'd said some terrible, injurious things to each other. But even as she'd packed her bag and stormed out of the house, she'd never expected it to end their marriage. She'd thought they'd needed a cooling-off period.

Somehow, though, cool had become frigid, then frozen. Frozen things shatter when dropped.

Divorce was the word, the sound of their frozen marriage hitting the ground.

"Well . . ." she began, then faltered for more to say.

One side of his mouth lifted in a grim smile. "Yeah, well. So did you know what she had in mind?"

"Suggesting we . . ." She couldn't make herself say the D-word, so she skipped it. "No. She told me she wanted us to spend Christmas together so that we wouldn't be tense and ill at ease with each other during the wedding."

"That's what she told me, too."

Silence fell between them now, with *awkward* and *tense* being the words of the day. Emma's throat closed up, and pressure built behind her eyes. *I will not cry. I will* not *cry!*

Jared drummed his fingers against the table. Emma felt the weight of his gaze on her, but she couldn't make herself return it. She feared that if she did when faced with the coldness in his eyes, she'd lose her battle against tears.

"So," he said abruptly. "How do you want to do this? Trade the names of our lawyers?"

The question was a knife plunging into her heart.

Trying hard not to betray the wound, she reached her right hand calmly for her water glass. Hidden beneath the table, the fingernails on her left hand dug into her thigh. A sip of water helped rid her of the lump in her throat. Left with only her pride, she managed to say, "Sure. I'll email that information to you first thing tomorrow."

His chin lifted slightly. "Okay. Good. I'll do the same."

"Okay. Good."

Jared pushed a miniature crab cake around his plate with his fork. "I don't want this to be ugly."

"I don't, either. I hope we can avoid that. I'll certainly try."

"Me, too."

Once again, the uncomfortable silence fell. Emma searched for something to say—anything—that would give her a legitimate excuse to leave. She wanted nothing more than to fling herself onto her bed and cry into her pillow.

Jared set down his fork and took a sip of water. "I guess we should tell Molly she's getting the gift she wanted."

"Yes." Emma licked her lips. "I know she worried we would make the wedding festivities awkward. She'll be happy to hear that we've settled everything."

His fingers tightened around his glass. *So, he isn't as calm as he pretended. Well, good.* As time ticked by, Emma experienced the sudden urge to throw away her pride and attempt to talk to him. Really talk to him.

The notion gained strength as he picked up his fork and resumed his meal. Emma rearranged her napkin. Words—honest words—bubbled up inside her, but before she could give them a voice, Jared said, "I'm glad we see eye to eye on this. It makes everything easier. So, have you met Mason's parents yet? They seem like very nice people."

Her stomach sank. They saw eye to eye. Well, guess that told her. She worked to keep her voice steady as she answered. "Yes, I like the Malones very much. So does Molly."

She heard the door behind her open, and she looked around, expecting to see Molly. Instead, she watched Celeste rush into the room. "I'm so sorry to interrupt, but we have a problem downstairs. Molly and I were rearranging a few things in the parlor in preparation for the bridal portraits you're scheduled to take in the morning. Unfortunately, she bumped into the Christmas tree. An ornament broke, and it's led to a bit of a meltdown. I think she could use a parental shoulder for support."

"I'll go," Jared said without hesitation. He set down his napkin, shoved back his chair, and fled the room without looking at Emma or speaking another word.

Just like that, the reunion dinner was done.

Sort of like our marriage.

Molly knew it was silly to lose it over a broken Christmas tree ornament, but she couldn't seem to help herself. That said ornament had been a puffed red heart hadn't helped. When she'd knelt on the parlor floor and began picking up the pieces, the metaphor moment had hit her like a fist.

When she'd first considered bringing up the topic of divorce, she'd known that her parents might jump at the suggestion. Her idea had not been a stab at reverse psychology; she sincerely believed the status quo needed to change. This limbo their family had existed in had dragged on long enough.

In hindsight, she recognized that a part of her had nursed the hope that they would reject the idea out of hand. That hadn't happened. Her parents' expressions in the wake of her request had shown stunned surprise and dismay, but not dismissal, dashing Molly's hopes. So, when she'd accidentally knocked the ornament off the parlor Christmas tree, her emotions had gone berserk.

Then her father had walked into the parlor looking as grim as the Grinch, and she'd needed no further confirmation. The divorce was on.

"Well, fine," she said, using anger to insulate against the pain as she changed into her pajamas a short time later. "Let them throw our family away. This time next week, I'll have a new family."

She cried herself to sleep and slept fitfully. She dreamed she was a rusted metal pinball bouncing through a forest of Christmas trees strung with blinking red lights. Glass ornaments shaped like brides and grooms hung from the branches. She banged into one tree. Bammed into another. Glass tinkled, then crackled and crashed. Shards of ornaments rained down upon the snow-covered ground where they lay like broken promises.

Pinball Molly didn't want to be rusty and hard. She wanted to be a bright, shiny, soft silver ball. A pretty ball that wouldn't break the brides and grooms. But her rusty ball rolled into a rabbit hole and fell and fell and fell . . . *Mommy! Daddy!*

"Molly?"

She pried her eyes open to sunshine and a sight and a scent that warmed her heart. Mason. Her Mason. Holding two steaming mugs of divinely aromatic coffee. "What time is it?" She rubbed the sleep from her eyes. "What are you doing here? How did you get into my room?"

The mattress dipped as he sat beside her. "I swiped your extra key card last night. You were so upset, and I wanted to check in on you. Actually, I wanted to *stay* with you, but we have too much family occupying rooms along this hallway for me to be comfortable with that."

She accepted the mug he offered, sniffed appreciatively, then took a reverent sip. As a delicious nutty flavor exploded on her tongue, memories of the previous evening flooded her brain, and her stomach lurched. The reunion dinner. Her suggestion. Her mother's brittle expression. Her somber father's distracted attempt to assure Molly that her sobs over the broken ornament had been a case of the bridal jitters. Molly—and Mason—had known better. Her not-so-little emotional outburst in the Angel's Rest parlor had nothing to do with getting married; it was all about the ending of one. "Oh, Mason. I'm so thankful that I have you. I don't know what I'd do without you."

"Luckily for us both, you'll never have to know." He tenderly tucked a strand of her hair behind her ear. "Now, how do you feel? Are you rested? We have a busy day ahead of us."

Beginning with my bridal portraits, Molly thought. *The morning after a major crying jag. What spectacular timing.*

"Do we need to reschedule some things?" Mason asked, watching her closely.

"No. I'll be fine. Thank heavens for Photoshop, though. And the fact that photography is my dad's hobby, and he's really good at it. My eyes feel as if sandpaper lines my lids. I'm afraid to look in the mirror."

"You're beautiful, Molly. I can't wait to see you in your wedding gown."

She gazed up at her fiancé, and her heart went gooey. They'd met by happenstance; the student ticket lottery having given them seats next to each other at the A&M vs. Missouri baseball game. The Aggies didn't win that game . . . but she'd hit a home run.

"I'm just as excited to see you in a tux." She glanced at the bedside clock, then leaned forward and kissed him. "However, neither one will happen today. Thank you for bringing me coffee and checking on me, but I guess I'd better get moving. I'm due at the spa for hair and makeup in twenty minutes."

He sipped his coffee and studied her. "You're really okay, honey?"

She took stock. Angry . . . frustrated . . . terribly sad, but . . . "I'm okay. I'll see you and your family at lunch. I can't wait to meet your Great-Uncle Fred."

"Don't remind me!" Mason closed his eyes and groaned. "I swear, if he takes out his teeth and wiggles his tongue at you, I'll deck him."

Following one last quick kiss, Mason exited the room, accompanied by Molly's laughter. But as soon as the door shut behind him, tears again flooded her eyes. *Stop it,* she told herself, throwing back the plump comforter and exiting the bed. *No more tears until after pictures.*

She showered and dressed and managed . . . barely . . . to greet her mother with a smile at the spa. To Molly's relief, when the topic of marriage entered the conversation, the only marriage under discussion was the one to be consecrated in St. Stephen's on the twenty-eighth. The hairdresser asked about Mason as she went to work on Molly's updo. The makeup artist brandished eye cream and drops he guaranteed would deal with the ravages of tears. Molly was able to shift her focus away from her parents and enjoy the experience of being pampered. By the time the makeup guy brushed gloss across her lips and pronounced her done, excitement had displaced much of Molly's anger.

Emma moved to stand behind her, and they both stared at Molly's reflection in the mirror. "You look gorgeous," Emma told her. "Simply gorgeous."

"She's a younger version of you, Emma," Celeste observed from the doorway. "You are both gorgeous women."

Emma gave a little laugh. "That's kind of you, Celeste. You are totally right about Molly, but, unfortunately, I feel more gargoyle than gorgeous today."

"That's just silly, Mom." Molly rose from her seat and, careful not to smudge makeup or muss hair, hugged her mother. "I was looking at your wedding pictures the last time I was home. If I can look half as good on my wedding day as you looked the day you married Dad, I'll be thrilled. You were the most beautiful bride I've ever seen."

"Now, who's being silly?"

"It's true. Aunt Shelby agreed with me when I said it." Following a significant pause, she added, "Dad did, too."

Emma's eyes rounded, and she briefly went still. Intrigued by the reaction, Molly expounded. "We were talking about the bridal portraits and wedding photos. I was putting together a list of the pictures I want to be taken during the ceremony and reception. Dad talked quite a bit about your wedding day."

"Oh," Emma said, a series of emotions fluttering

across her expression—surprise, curiosity, pain. "Well . . . hmm . . . I'd better go settle the bill."

She hurried off, leaving Molly staring after her, tapping her toes in frustration. Celeste moved to Molly's side and linked their arms. "Honey, is there anything else I can do for you this morning?"

Molly thought about the contents of the closet in her room. After graduation, she'd spent a few days at the Wildcatter, where she'd made a spur-of-the-moment addition to her luggage before leaving for Eternity Springs. "You know what? I do believe there is. If you're free for the next half hour or so, I could use some help with something." Narrowing her eyes, she watched her mother sign a credit card receipt and added, "I have a surprise for my parents."

Outside of Angel's Rest's front parlor, Emma hesitated and braced herself. *You can do this. You've been performing for years. This is what you do. You're a professional.* Pasting a smile onto her face, she stepped into the room. "Good morning, Jared."

He stood in front of one of the room's tall windows, gazing out onto the estate's snow-covered grounds. She detected a slight stiffening of his spine before he turned. "Hello, Emma. Is Molly almost ready?"

"Actually, I don't know. Celeste is helping her dress. Molly banished me from her bedroom. She said she wants to make an entrance—with a capital *E*."

Jared nodded. "Sounds like Molly."

"She said she's afraid she'll be too nervous to notice our reaction when we first see her on her . . ." Emma paused as her cell phone ringtone sounded. She pulled the phone from the pocket of her slacks, then finished her sentence with a distracted murmur: " . . . wedding day. Excuse me, I need to take this call." She thumbed the green button and said, "Hello, Nicco. I'm so glad to hear from you. Did you get my message?"

Emma turned away, but not before she saw Jared's jaw go hard.

"Yes, I got your message. I have already been by your apartment to pick up your green Loubi's," said Nicco. "They are in my suitcase. I cannot believe you forgot to pack them."

"Me, either." The Christian Louboutin shoes completed her mother-of-the-bride outfit.

"However, *bella,* I am not calling about your shoes. I have a boon to ask of you. I know it is very late, but do you have room for one more guest at the wedding? Would you be terribly inconvenienced if I brought my fiancée?"

"Of course, we have room for one more guest . . . wait." Emma gasped with delight. "Did you say your fiancée? Nicco! You asked Francesca to marry you?"

"And she accepted."

"Of course, she accepted! She loves you. Oh, Nicco. I'm so happy for you both."

"She wants to surprise her parents with the news in

person on New Year's, so she's traveling west with me. We'll go on to San Francisco after Molly's wedding."

"I'm so thrilled, Nicco. Molly will be, too."

"And how is the blushing bride? And, of course, I want to hear all about your reunion with the big bad wolf."

Emma cut her gaze toward Jared. He'd abandoned any pretense of not listening. "Jared is about to take Molly's bridal portrait. We're waiting for her to make her grand entrance now."

"So, the man is standing right there?"

"Absolutely."

"In that case, you may give me a full recounting at a later date. I'll see you the day after Christmas, Emma. Do you need me to bring anything else?"

"No. Bring my shoes, and I'll be set. Travel safely, Nicco, and please pass along my congratulations to Francesca."

Emma disconnected the call, then slipped her phone back into the pocket of her slacks. She lifted her chin and met her husband's gaze in a silent dare. An emotion she couldn't quite place flitted across his face. Uncertainty? Regret? Confusion? Was he finally ready to admit that he believed her past denials about the nature of her relationship with Nicco?

The opportunity to confront the subject evaporated when Celeste swept into the room. "She'll be down in just a minute. I've ensured that Mason is out of the house, so the coast is clear."

Emma shifted her thoughts away from her dying

marriage to Molly and the marriage being born. She moved out into the hallway and took up a position with a good view of the second-floor landing. Jared stood beside her. It was the closest the two of them had been in well over three years. He asked, "She told me the two of you shopped for her dress."

"Yes. We met in Dallas in September."

"She says it's a princess gown."

Emma appreciated that they could still talk to each other about their daughter. She and Jared might end their marriage, but shared parenthood would continue for the rest of their lives. "It's definitely a statement dress. I thought she'd go with something sleek and sophisticated, but the instant the saleslady showed her this one, she fell in love."

"I want her to be happy," Jared said, his voice gruff with emotion. "That's all I really care about."

"I know. I do, too."

Movement above them snagged Emma's attention, and she looked up. The slow smile that spread across her face abruptly froze. *Oh, Molly.* Emma inhaled sharply as Jared rested his hand on her shoulder. "Isn't that—?"

"My wedding gown," Emma murmured, instinctively lifting her hand to rest atop her husband's. "Yes."

The dress was a sleek strapless A-line satin gown with an embroidered floral cutout lined with sheer organza, sequins, and beads—and looked nothing like the full-skirted tulle creation Molly had chosen at the bridal shop in Dallas.

"She takes my breath away," Jared said. "She looks just like you, Emma."

Emma blinked back the tears that stung her eyes at his words and watched silently as their daughter reached the bottom of the staircase and produced a theatrical curtsy. "Ta-da! So, how do I look?"

"Absolutely gorgeous," Jared said, his voice gruff.

"Lovely, of course," Emma added. "But, Molly . . . I don't understand. I thought you loved your princess dress."

"I do. It's the prettiest dress ever. I am wearing it for my wedding."

"So why this?"

"It's symbolic. This dress represents your marriage, and I'm the product of that marriage, so I wanted a photograph of me wearing this dress. Before, well..." Molly waved her hand in a small circle, silently saying, "Before it's over."

Before. Emma shut her eyes.

Molly shrugged and continued, "I'd like you to take a few shots of me in this dress, then I'll change into mine. Okay, Dad?"

"Whatever you want, honey."

Inside the parlor, Jared adjusted the lights while Molly rattled on about her recent visit to the ranch. "I'm so glad I decided to poke around in the attic and discovered your gown, Mom. It's a little short for me—I have Dad's height—but except for that, it fits perfectly. It's a beautiful dress, Mom. Maybe someday, my daughter will have her photograph taken while wearing it. I think that would be so cool."

Emma couldn't speak past the lump in her throat, so she smiled wanly and nodded.

Jared directed Molly to stand in front of the Christmas tree. He took a dozen or more photos, and the room's mood grew somber with each pose. It didn't help that Molly decided this was the perfect time to begin a session of "remember when." Finally, even Jared seemed to have had enough. "I have some really great shots, honey. Why don't you change into your other dress now?"

"Okay. Except first . . . Celeste . . . would you mind? I'd like a picture of the three of us while I'm wearing this dress."

"Oh, honey," Emma protested. "I'm not dressed for photographs."

"It won't be for your adoring fans, Mother. This is strictly for me. One last family portrait."

One last family portrait. Emma shut her eyes.

"Molly . . ." Jared began, but when he faltered, Celeste stepped up and took charge. Before Emma quite realized what was going on, Celeste had positioned them in front of the Christmas tree in the inn's front parlor. Emma was standing on her daughter's right, Jared to Molly's left.

Celeste prattled on about portraits while she snapped off photos with a camera that looked as fancy as Jared's. Celeste could have been employed as a Broadway choreographer judging by how she posed, propped, and directed hands and feet to hold here and move there. Before Emma caught her breath, the family photos had been taken. Celeste and Molly had quit the room, and she and Jared were alone again.

He kept stealing glances at her. Finally, she'd had enough. "What is it?"

He obviously wrestled with what he intended to say, and Emma braced herself, confident she wouldn't like it. Finally, Jared sighed. "She sure knows how to pull our strings, doesn't she? One last family portrait starring your wedding gown? She's angry with us and pretending not to be. Tell you something else, we should probably have the real photographer do another round of portraits. My camera lens didn't lie, and she couldn't hide her emotions. I don't think she will like what she sees once these portraits are finished."

Emma nodded. "I'll talk to the photographer."

Jared's attention didn't waver from her, so Emma raised a brow. "Is there something else?"

"She looks so much like you, Emma. Seeing her today in that dress . . . it takes me back. It makes me feel twenty years old again. Twenty going on two hundred."

"She's a lovely young woman, Jared, inside and out. We can be proud."

"Yes. I only wish that Molly could be as proud of us."

Sadly, Emma had no comeback for that observation. Silence fell between them, the only sounds those Jared made as he readjusted his camera equipment. When Celeste hurried into the room a few minutes later with a harried look on her face, Emma seized upon the distraction. "Celeste, has something bad happened?"

"Yes, I'm afraid so. I just received a call from our secretary at St. Stephens with some distressing news. Kelly Green slipped on ice on the church steps after the morning service. She broke her ankle, and it puts us in a pickle."

Emma tried to recall if she knew Kelly Green. The name sounded familiar, but she couldn't place it.

Celeste met Jared's curious gaze and explained. "Besides being the secretary at St. Stephen's, Kelly is Eternity Springs' one and only pianist."

Oh. Now Emma remembered. Molly and Mason had an appointment on the calendar tomorrow to discuss music choices for the ceremony.

"She doesn't want you to worry," Celeste assured them. "She'll be able to play for Molly's wedding—even though just between us, she's nervous about playing in front of you, Emma—but she's had painkillers today and can't play tonight. There's no one to take her place."

Jared asked, "What's happening tonight?"

"Our community school is putting on their Christmas pageant tonight." Celeste looked at Emma and smiled encouragingly. "We'd be ever so grateful if you'd take her place. One of our more affluent residents donated a fabulous piano to the school. You need not worry about being forced to play a clunker. The children will be crushed if they're not able to perform."

"I'll be happy to pitch in," Emma responded.

"Wonderful." Celeste turned to Jared. "We also need someone to be our official photographer since that job was assigned to Kelly's husband. He'll need to stay with his wife tonight. Can we count on your help, too?"

Jared gave Celeste an easy smile, markedly different from any he'd shown toward Emma. "Sure."

Celeste clapped her hands. "Wonderful. Thank you so much. Molly is on her way down again, but I have something to show you first." She removed a wooden box from one of the parlor bookcases. "After seeing her gown, I realized I have the perfect accessory to loan her, but I wouldn't offer it before asking you first. If the little pearl clip attached to her veil has special meaning to one of you, I'll simply put this away."

"The clip isn't anything special," Emma replied. "It's costume jewelry."

"Well, this isn't. It was a gift from a friend. I save it for special occasions. It's fitting for both a princess and an angel, so I think it's perfect for Molly on her wedding day."

"An angel?" Jared murmured.

"She has a true and loving heart. No matter how old Molly gets or where life takes her, she will always be your little angel, will she not?" When Jared and Emma nodded, Celeste added, "I would be proud if she wore this on her wedding day."

She opened the box and revealed a diamond-studded tiara in a pattern reminiscent of an angel's wings. "Oh, Celeste," Emma murmured. "It's fabulous. You'll make her the happiest bride ever."

"No," the other woman replied. "That job is up to Mason and"—she gave them each a significant look in turn—"to the two of you."

The tears that spilled down Emma's cheeks a minute later had little to do with the princess bride who floated into the drawing room to have her picture taken.

After the portrait session, Jared declined an invitation to join the Malone family for lunch. He spent the afternoon cross-country skiing, exercising, and exorcising his demons—or attempting to, anyway. He allowed himself to think about his relationship with Emma, something he'd not permitted himself to do for a very long time. He returned to Angel's Rest in a pensive mood.

Marital mistakes were sorry thoughts to carry into a children's Christmas program. That's why Jared tried to focus on happier times as he gathered his camera bag from the backseat of his car and walked through the frigid night air toward the school that evening. But when he walked into the auditorium, accepted a program from a kindergartner dressed like an elf, and heard his wife playing "Greensleeves" on an upright piano, sadness overwhelmed him.

The first picture he snapped was one of Emma at the piano.

The program introduced an original play written by the sixth-grade class, followed by a Christmas carol sing-along. Eavesdropping on a conversation between a woman named Nic and one called Sage, he learned that the play was a version of the Nativity story as it had never been told before. The house lights dimmed, and Jared turned his attention to the stage.

The first-grader dressed in a white choir robe and sporting gold paper-mâché wings was a doll who reminded him so much of Molly at that age that Jared's heart hurt.

The storyline centered on a trio of angels announcing the birth of the Savior. One of them, Harold, was distracted by offerings at the bazaar of Bethlehem and was late heralding the news to the Three Kings, who decided to trade in their camels for faster transportation.

Jared almost dropped his camera when he saw the scene for that part of the story. Three boys dressed in kingly gear sat perched atop stuffed animals—not the plush kind, but the work of a taxidermist—a bear, a mountain lion, and a bighorn sheep.

Seeing Jared's surprise, Celeste leaned over and whispered, "The school owns quite an extensive collection of preserved wildlife donated by a former resident of Eternity Springs."

On stage, the youngest angel clasped her hands and dramatically despaired, "What's Christmas without camels?"

The audience erupted in laughter, and Jared grinned, snapping a shot of the young drama queen he knew her parents would treasure.

Onstage, the Three Kings realized they still weren't going to make it to the manger in time, and at that point, the materialistic little cherubim saw the light. Harold flew the kings on Angel Airlines, delivering them to the stable in time to honor the Christ Child. Unfortunately, Angel Air lost the kings' baggage, so they despaired that they had no gold, frankincense, or myrrh to give the newborn King. At that point, angel Harold patted them on the back and said, "Hark. I say unto you. It's the thought that counts."

It was silly and sappy, but the little drama provided the first spark of Christmas cheer Jared had enjoyed all year. Then the lights dimmed, and the three angels took center stage beneath a spotlight. Taking a page from Linus and *A Charlie Brown Christmas,* they took turns reciting lines from the second chapter of the Gospel of St. Luke. All the performers recited the final lines, "Glory to God in the highest, and on earth peace and goodwill toward men."

Then the stage lights flashed bright, and the entire cast declared, "And that's what Christmas is all about, Eternity Springs!"

Emma played the introduction to "Joy to the World," and the sing-along commenced.

Soon, peace and goodwill settled over Jared like a snowfall. Without conscious thought, he drifted toward the piano. He'd always loved listening to Emma play, but being near and watching her . . . what a turn-on. She played the piano with such passion, such emotion, and those times when she'd held his gaze and spoken to him through her music—wow. More than once, he'd grabbed her up and taken her there against the piano.

He couldn't believe they'd never share such moments again.

He didn't plan to move beside her. Nevertheless, that's where he ended up. When Emma glanced up and saw him, her eyes widened. Then, to his surprise, she smiled.

Jared stayed.

Eventually, the sing-along ended. A man who introduced himself as the mayor stepped up to the microphone and publicly thanked Emma for pitching in to help. A practiced performer, she took her bows. As the audience filed out of the auditorium, she turned back to the piano and started to stack the sheet music. Acting instinctively, Jared said, "Taking requests?"

Again, she showed him that smile, and Jared's sense of goodwill intensified. "What would you like to hear?"

"The Schumann."

She hesitated, and he thought she was going to refuse. But then she closed her eyes, and her fingers began to move. The sound of "Träumerei" rose and filled his heart and soul, and as he watched her sway and move with the passion of the piece, his blood heated.

Her eyes opened. Their gazes met and held. It was a dance they'd performed time and time again. It was their dance.

Time hung suspended. He didn't see the stragglers in the audience being hurried along toward the reception in the gymnasium on the other side of the school by Celeste and Molly. He didn't realize the house lights had dimmed or that he and Emma were alone together. He was aware only of the music, the heavy-lidded warmth in Emma's eyes, and the yearning that filled him.

He wished the song could last forever, but the piece progressed to its inevitable end. Emma closed her eyes and played the final bars. As the last note echoed through the auditorium and died away, Jared felt as if he stood on a precipice.

Three little words floated through his mind. Was it too late? What would happen if he said them? Did he want to say *Emma come home*?

He hesitated too long, and Emma broke the spell. Standing, she picked up her purse. "It's been a long day, and I'm tired. I think I'll skip the reception and head back to Angel's Rest. Good night, Jared."

She was almost to the door before he found his voice. "Thank you, Emma. For the song."

She paused. "I enjoyed playing for you."

As her footsteps faded, Jared released a heavy, sad sigh. He and Emma had just said their goodbyes.

As Christmas approached, Molly grew both more excited and more despairing. She loved all the hustle and bustle surrounding the holiday and wedding preparations. She hated how her mom and dad managed to participate in the said hustle and bustle and yet seldom interacted. She guessed that this was what she had to look forward to from now on, where her parents were concerned.

They weren't happy. Maybe divorce really was the right thing for them. This state of suspension wasn't good for anybody. Seeing them together but still apart hurt Molly's heart. Maybe she'd made a mistake asking for one last family Christmas. Maybe she and Mason should have eloped.

A knock on the door of her room at Angel's Rest interrupted her brooding. "Come in."

The door cracked open, and her dad stuck his head inside. "Hey, sweetheart. Got a little time for your old man?"

"Sure. I don't meet Mason for another twenty minutes." She and the Malones had reservations for an afternoon sleigh ride around Hummingbird Lake.

Her father entered the room carrying a shopping bag filled with packages wrapped in Christmas paper. "Can I get you to do a favor for me, Molly?"

"Sure. What's up?"

He held up the bag. "These are for your mother. They've piled up over the past few years, and I'd like you to give them to her for me."

Molly straightened in alarm. "You're not leaving, are you? You'll be here for Christmas?"

"Yes. I promised you I'd be here, and I'm not going to weasel out."

"Then why don't you give her the gifts?"

He shrugged. "I don't think it's appropriate at this point."

"Why not? What are they?"

"Just some things I thought she could use."

"But, Dad, I don't understand. Are you not going to give her a Christmas gift this year?"

"I'm going to give her a gift," he said with a scowl. "Just not these gifts."

"Why not?"

The exasperated look on his face told her he would say no more about it. "I need to run. I'm picking up your grandmother and aunt at the airport in Gunnison at four. Have fun on your sleigh ride this afternoon."

After he left, she inspected the bag and recognized the wrapping paper on the box on top. It was the reindeer paper she'd bought last year to wrap his gifts for Nana and Aunt Shelby. She picked up the second box and studied it. The gold foil struck a memory, too. She'd brought that paper home for the holidays from college two years ago. The third box . . . she remembered that one sitting beneath the Christmas tree the first year that her mother didn't come home.

Molly sat cross-legged on her bed and stared at the packages. He'd kept buying Mom gifts. He'd kept buying her gifts, and he'd brought them to give to her this Christmas.

That had to mean something, didn't it?

She thought about it during the sleigh ride, and it was still on her mind when she met her mom for a mother-daughter dinner. She wanted to tell Mom about the gifts, but she thought it best to work the conversation around to that topic carefully.

First, she brought up plans for Christmas Eve. The Stapleton family tradition was to open gifts after the midnight church service. "Are you sure you don't mind attending church with the Malones on Christmas Eve, Mom?"

"Not at all, honey. They're a lovely family, and I think it will be good to have extra people around."

"Mason says they don't exchange gifts until Christmas morning."

Emma set down her fork, then sipped her water. "I've wanted to talk to you about that, honey. I don't think an after-church Christmas exchange is right for us this year."

It was as good an opening as Molly figured she would get. "You don't have a gift for Dad?"

"I have a gift." Emma's lips twisted ruefully. "I have more than one gift, in fact."

"Really?" As far as Molly knew, her parents never did multiple gifts. They believed a one-person/one-gift rule kept the season from getting out of hand.

"I have last year's gift, too. I brought his gift for the years we haven't been together."

Now it was Molly's turn to set down her fork. "You've continued to buy him gifts? Even though you weren't speaking to him?"

"I always thought maybe . . ." Emma's voice trailed off. "Well, that doesn't matter anymore. I'm happy to go to church with you and your father on Christmas Eve, Molly, but I cannot do a traditional family gift exchange. Frankly, I'm a little too emotional right now for that. All right?"

"Sure, Mom."

Later that night, as she met Mason and Lori at the hot springs for a nighttime dip, she told them about her parents and their Christmas gifts. "They both continued to buy Christmas gifts for each other even though they weren't speaking. Don't you think that's significant?"

"You know your parents better than we do," Mason said.

Lori sank into the bubbling hot water up to her neck, then looked above to the star-filled sky. "I think it's significant. I think it shows they still care for each other."

"I agree," Molly replied. "I just don't know what to do about it. They still don't talk. Not about important stuff, anyway. They talk about the weather. They are polite to each other. It breaks my heart."

The trio sat quietly as they thought about the issue. Then, after a few minutes, Lori said, "Why don't you ask my mom and her friends for advice? This sort of thing is right up their alley. They do relationship 'interventions' at the drop of a hat."

Molly glanced at Mason, silently asking his opinion. He took her hand and said, "I don't see what it would hurt."

"Okay," Molly said. "But I'm running out of time. When do you think I could talk to them?"

"Come for breakfast tomorrow. Eight o'clock. That's usually the best time to get everyone together. I'll talk to Mom tonight, and if there is any problem, I'll text you."

"Sounds like a plan," Molly said.

That's how she and her maid of honor ended up in Lori's mother's kitchen on the twenty-third of December with Sarah Reese and her best friends— Ali Timberlake, Sage Rafferty, and Nic Callahan. As Sarah set a coffee cake fresh from the oven in the center of the table, a knock sounded on the door. Sarah waved Celeste Blessing inside.

"I'm sorry I'm late," Celeste said as she unwrapped a gold knit scarf from around her neck and shrugged out of her coat. As she hung them on a hook in the mudroom, she added, "Mason's mother stopped me to inquire about some last-minute arrangements for the rehearsal dinner. So, what did I miss?"

"Nothing," Sarah replied, handing Celeste a steaming mug of coffee. "We haven't started yet."

"I just arrived myself," Sage added.

"Excellent." Celeste smiled warmly toward Molly and said, "So, dear girl, how can we help you?"

"I'm looking for advice. My parents are on the brink of divorce, and I'm pretty sure they're making a mistake." She told them about the gifts, then said, "I think this is wrong. I think they still love each other, and I don't know what to do about it."

"What happened to bring them to this point?" Sarah asked. "Celeste and I have heard part of it, but why don't you start at the beginning and give all of us the whole scoop?"

"Okay." The story poured out of Molly. She told them about her dad and uncle being teammates and how Uncle Frank had been Jared's best man at his wedding. "Both my folks said that he had a brilliant mind for business. After my Grandpa Stapleton died, they thought bringing Uncle Frank on as the Wildcatter's business manager was a great idea. It *was* a great idea until Uncle Frank embezzled money from the ranch."

"Oh, no," Ali said.

"Yeah. Dad had a horse who could really run, and he got the Wildcatter involved in horse racing. That's how Uncle Frank caught the gambling bug. Apparently, he lost everything but couldn't stop gambling, and he eventually stole a lot of money from the Wildcatter accounts. After Dad discovered what was happening, he confronted Uncle Frank. They had a terrible fight, and later that night, my uncle went into the bunkhouse and shot himself."

Sarah gave Molly a comforting hug. Sage Rafferty said, "Oh, how terrible for your family."

"It was awful," Molly said, recalling the phone call she'd received late one winter night. "I was away at school, and my Aunt Shelby called to tell me what happened. My parents were too shaken up. They were devastated, both of them. Dad was furious; my mom was totally brokenhearted. Her parents were already gone, and her brother had been her only living relative."

"That's what led to their estrangement?" Nic asked.

"Yes. I think so, anyway. I came home for the funeral, and they acted okay. But it obviously wasn't okay because they hardly talked to each other the next time I came home. Not long after that, Mom left to go on tour, and she never came back."

Celeste sipped her coffee, then set down her mug. "But you truly believe they are still in love?"

"I do! I do think they love each other, but neither one has been willing to make the first move to make things right again."

"I almost hate to ask," Sarah said, "but what about that gorgeous Italian who came to your graduation with your mother?"

"That's Nicco. He and Mom aren't together. He's engaged to someone else. He is Mom's manager, that's all." When she saw Nic and Ali share a doubting glance, she added, "It's true. I asked my mom. She said she still considers herself a married woman, and she's never been unfaithful to Dad. She doesn't lie to me."

"What about your dad?" Lori asked. "Does he have a girlfriend?"

"No. He doesn't do anything but work. I don't think he's left the Wildcatter a dozen times since my uncle died. I think they came really close to losing the ranch."

"Well, then." Celeste drummed her fingers against the tabletop. "I think we should help this marriage heal, don't you, my friends?"

"Absolutely," Ali replied. "I know from personal experience that marriages can survive rough spots and end up stronger and happier than ever."

"Cool," Nic said. "Another intervention." She

winked at Molly and added, "They've become a habit of ours."

Sage took a bite of coffee cake, then gestured with her fork as she said, "Since your parents are not spending time together, I guess that would be our task."

"We could lock them in the basement at Angel's Rest together," Sarah suggested. "That worked for Nic and Gabe."

Nic's smile went smug. "It was very romantic."

"I'm afraid we have too many people in residence now," Celeste said. "Someone would be certain to let them out."

"Locking them in a room together someplace is a great idea," Sage agreed.

Molly's mouth gaped, and she looked at Lori. "Your mom and her friends are awesome."

"I know," Lori replied.

"What about your restaurant, Ali?" Sarah asked. "Is your basement a possibility?"

Ali's teeth nibbled her bottom lip as she thought it over. "As a last resort, maybe. It would depend on the timing. I have a lot of prep work for the food for the wedding reception."

"I don't think we'll need it," Celeste said, sitting up straight. A delighted smile spread across her face. "I think if our handyman at Angel's Rest could find time to make a few special arrangements for us, I know the perfect place."

Sage asked, "What can my husband do to help? I'm volunteering him right now."

"I just love teamwork," Nic added. "And I love Celeste's plans. Her A-for-Angel plan, which brought Eternity Springs back from the precipice of ruin was a rousing success. So, what do you have in mind this time?"

Celeste picked a piece of pecan off the coffee cake and popped it into her mouth. "Plan B, of course."

"Plan B for Bride?" Lori asked.

"Almost. I'm thinking plan B for . . ." Celeste paused dramatically, then made a flourishing gesture with her hands toward Molly and spoke triumphantly: "Bridezilla!"

"What in the world happened to my sweet, laid-back, I-don't-care-as-long-as-the-people-I-love-are-here, bride-to-be daughter?" Emma asked Jared as they left Ali Timberlake's restaurant on Christmas Eve after making the final arrangements for the reception meal. "She's like a different person."

"She is acting a bit . . . high-strung," he conceded.

"High-strung? High-strung!" Emma lifted her face toward the sky. "She's a raving lunatic! Why in the world would she think it's okay to change the flower arrangements less than a week before the wedding? Maybe if we were in Denver, but we're not! We're in Eternity Springs! You know, I adore Lori Reese. I truly do. But why in heaven's name did she think it was a good idea to suggest to our daughter that she needed mistletoe as part of her decorations at this late date?"

"It's annoying, I'll agree."

Emma was still fuming twenty minutes later when Jared pulled his car into one of the remote parking lots at Angel's Rest. "Where are we going? I didn't listen to Celeste's directions while Molly was in the middle of her manicotti meltdown."

"That way." He pointed in the direction of a tree-lined path that led toward the mountain rising behind Angel's Rest.

"Where does it lead?"

"An abandoned mine."

Emma pursed her lips. "And we are walking toward an abandoned mine why?"

"It's not exactly abandoned. Celeste says it's actually a natural cave that miners expanded. She reclaimed it for storage—said she had engineers look it over, so it's safe. Apparently, she has some Christmas decorations stored there that she decided not to use at Angel's Rest. Including a whole bunch of mistletoe harvested from the forest."

"Oh," Emma replied, relieved. "I was afraid she'd have us tromping through the snow harvesting the stuff ourselves. Do you know why she was so adamant that you and I get the mistletoe instead of somebody else?"

"Nope. I was going to ask you the same question."

Emma was suspicious of their daughter's motives, but she wasn't about to voice it. No way on God's snowy earth would she bring up the subject of kissing beneath the mistletoe to Jared Stapleton. Not when she was about to walk into a small, dark place with him to retrieve said plants.

Jared grabbed a flashlight from his car and led the way along the path. An inch of new snow had fallen overnight, and as they approached the trail, Emma noted that they were not the first people who had traveled in this direction today. She spied three distinct sets of boot prints. At least she didn't see any bear tracks. Or mountain lion tracks. Or wolf prints. Were there wolves in this part of the world? She didn't know.

She walked a little closer to Jared.

They didn't speak as they hiked up the gently sloping path. The mood between the two of them was comfortable and companionable. When was the last time Emma had felt this at ease with Jared? Not since that horrible night when they'd fought so bitterly. In that instant, Emma decided she was glad that Molly had insisted on this family time before the wedding. A little something inside her was healing.

The aroma of juniper and pine swirled in the gentle breeze. Movement off to her right caught Emma's attention, and she smiled in delight to see a fox spiriting through the woods.

Jared's voice broke the stillness of the forest. "Emma, do you think she's having second thoughts about going through with the wedding?"

The question put a damper on her enjoyment of the hike. She considered the idea, then shook her head. "I don't think so, but honestly, I don't know what's going on in her brain."

"What will we do if she wants to call it off?"

Emma shrugged. "It's her life. Her decision to make. But I don't think that will happen, Jared. She loves Mason."

His vaporized breath floated on the crisp mountain air with a note of bitterness to it. "Love doesn't necessarily keep a female from doing something stupid, does it?"

Well. That verbal arrow had come flying out of nowhere, hadn't it? Her spine went stiff, and she stared straight ahead, not responding to the barbed question. Then Jared surprised her by saying, "I'm sorry. I didn't mean that like it sounded."

Emma acknowledged the rare apology with a nod. "I think we're witnessing a full-blown case of bridal jitters. Molly will calm down."

"I sure hope so. Our daughter is driving me crazy." At that point, he paused and gestured up the trail. "Looks like we've arrived."

Emma saw a large wooden door sitting on wheeled tracks that passed in front of a shadowed opening in the mountainside. "I admit I find it a bit strange that Celeste would use a mountain cave for storage. What's wrong with the basement?"

"Maybe it's full," Jared replied, shrugging. He switched on his flashlight. "She's a strange sort of woman. I like her, though."

"Me, too."

Jared led the way into the cave, with Emma following a little closer than before. She wasn't claustrophobic or anything. She just wasn't one hundred percent sure that they weren't invading something's home. Her husband must have had a similar thought because he shined the flashlight around the chamber.

The natural cave was larger than she had expected. Better equipped, too, she realized, when he flipped a switch and electric lights lit the space. The far wall was boarded up, and DANGER—MINE ENTRANCE—NO ADMITTANCE signs hung on either side of a stack of metal shelving filled with boxes and baskets and . . . mistletoe. Lots and lots of mistletoe.

"It's everywhere," Jared said, staring above him.

Emma followed the path of his gaze to a latticework of rafters hung with dozens of sprigs of mistletoe, wrapped and hanging by strips of red velvet ribbon. "Somebody went to a lot of work."

"How much of this do you think she'll want?"

"Knowing Molly, most of it. I think we should—" Emma broke off abruptly when she spied the tray holding a bottle of champagne, two glasses, and an envelope with the words *Mom and Dad* penned across the front in Molly's handwriting. "Uh-oh."

"What?"

Before she could answer, a loud screeching sound filled the chamber, and the natural light disappeared. Emma's and Jared's heads whipped toward the entrance . . . where the door was slamming shut.

"What the hell?" Jared exclaimed. In two steps, he

was at the door, yanking back on the handle . . . to no avail.

At that point, Emma knew for sure. This had been one whole elaborate ruse. She marched over to the envelope and grabbed it. "That little sneak."

Jared's stare fastened on the paper. "She set us up, didn't she?"

Emma scanned the sheet. "I'm going to wring her neck."

"What does it say?"

She read aloud: "'Dear Mom and Dad. One of my first memories of Christmas is of the two of you locking lips beneath the mistletoe, so I know that you are not unaware of this particular tradition. What you might not know is a little piece of mistletoe history I discovered. You've always made me proud of my Scandinavian heritage, but never more so than now. Mom, Dad, are you aware that in Scandinavia, mistletoe was considered to be a plant of peace, and that under the mistletoe, enemies could declare a truce, and . . .'" Emma glanced up and met Jared's gaze. "She underlined *and* three times. 'And underneath the mistletoe, warring spouses can kiss and make up. It's true. I read it on *Wikipedia*.'"

Jared groaned aloud.

Emma continued reading. "'So, Mom and Dad, aka Stubborn and Intractable, here's your chance. You are under the mistletoe, and neither of you has to surrender. All you have to do is call a truce and talk. You haven't talked to each other—really talked—in years. Don't you think it's time you did? That's the real gift you can give me for Christmas. Do that, and I'll know, and you'll know that divorce truly is the right step for you. Do this, Mom and Dad, if not for yourselves, then for me. Please? Take advantage of this Christmas season and the message we all heard at the Christmas pageant the other night—peace on earth and goodwill toward men. Take advantage of the mistletoe. You may as well. And ask each other about the Christmas gifts you bought for each other. You have two hours to kill. Love, Molly.'"

"Time to kill?" Jared muttered. "What about a daughter?"

Emma lifted her gaze from the letter and looked at her husband. Really looked at him. He had his hands shoved into his coat pockets, and his jaw set defensively. But there was something in his eyes—a look that told her he wasn't entirely against the idea of a talk.

She realized that neither was she.

Emma took a deep breath and took the first step. "We shouldn't allow her to manipulate us this way."

"You're probably right," he replied.

"Probably," she emphasized.

A corner of his mouth quirked up. "Probably."

That was a tease, the first one she'd seen from him in forever. Since long before Frank died, certainly. Emma's pulse began to pound.

She waited. She'd taken the first step, right? He could darn well take the next one. She folded her arms and made a significant glance toward the ceiling.

He shocked her speechless when he took two bold

steps forward, then swooped in to kiss her once, briefly but firmly, on the mouth. "Pax, Emma."

She closed her eyes. The spark of hope within her flickered into a flame. She licked her lips and tasted him. "Pax, Jared."

Stepping away, he said, "Where do we start?"

She released a heavy sigh. "I guess everything started with Frank."

Frank.

The old feelings rolled through Jared at the sound of his brother-in-law's name. Anger. Fury. The sting of betrayal. The passage of time had dulled them to some extent, but they were far from extinguished. "I don't want to talk about your brother."

Emma's chest rose as she drew in a deep breath. "I think that's been part of the problem."

Jared winced. She was right. They'd had one rip-roaring fight and never discussed the situation again. "I'm still angry at him, Emma."

"So am I. He wronged both of us terribly, but that doesn't mean I don't mourn him. That doesn't mean that I don't still love him."

Jared's mouth flattened into a grim smile. "Loving someone doesn't preclude being furious at him."

To his surprise, Emma laughed. "Yes, Jared, I know."

He met her gaze and saw warmth in her big blue

eyes, and his tension eased. Hope lifted his heart. "What is it that you want to say about Frank?"

"Will you listen to me this time, Jared? Really listen to me?"

This was his chance, he realized. It was their chance. If they didn't make it through this conversation, he knew they'd never reconcile.

"Yes, I'll listen."

She blew out a heavy breath. "Okay, then. The first thing I want to say is that I apologize. It was wrong of me to try to hide Frank's problem from you. I was an enabler, and in the end, that hurt my brother worse than doing nothing and allowing the truth to come out sooner."

Exactly. Jared kept the thought to himself. He knew that giving it a voice would be counterproductive at this point.

"However," Emma continued, "I won't apologize for giving him the money to pay back the Wildcatter. My parents would have wanted me to do that with the proceeds from their life insurance policies. Giving Frank the money wasn't a mistake. Giving the money to Frank directly so he could gamble that away, too, was a bad decision."

"Can I say something about that? Will you listen to me, too?" When she nodded, he continued: "I wasn't angry that you gave him the money, Emma. It was your money to give. It was the lie that I couldn't abide by. You protected him rather than protecting me."

"Because I didn't tell you that my brother stole money from the Wildcatter?"

"Yes." *She finally got it!*

"Don't you see, Jared? I thought I was protecting you both. You loved Frank just as much as I did. Honestly, maybe more. You two might not have been related by blood, but you were a true brother to Frank. I knew you'd be devastated to learn he'd stolen from you."

"Not just from me but from my family. Emma, we almost lost the Wildcatter. Only the grace of God and a banker who bucked his board to work with me kept that from happening."

"I'm so sorry, Jared. I'm so terribly sorry that my brother's addiction cost you so much."

"He cost *us,*" Jared continued, the words he'd wanted to say for so long spewing out of him as he paced the cave's confines like a caged mountain lion. "He cost Molly. If the man wasn't already dead, I'd kill him for what he did to us! He was such a freaking coward to take his own life!"

"Yes, he was."

Jared closed his eyes and fought back the bitterness. He wouldn't let Frank ruin this opportunity. "I was so angry at him for killing himself."

"You were angry at Frank, angry at me."

"Angry at myself. I couldn't mourn him, Emma."

"I know. I was angry at you because of that. I missed him so much. I lost my brother, and all you could think about was saving the cursed Wildcatter."

He raked his fingers through his hair. "I'm sorry, Emma."

"You weren't there for me when I needed you most."

"That was wrong of me. I'm so very sorry."

She smiled sadly as tears glistened in her eyes. "*I'm sorry* are such powerful words. Why was saying them so hard for us? Why has it taken us so long to say them?"

"Because we're . . . How did Molly put it? Stubborn and intractable." He moved slowly toward his wife, saying, "I also think we were lost in our own pain, coming at it from two directions. We should have been strong enough to be there for each other. You are right, honey. *I'm sorry* are powerful words, and we are a pair of fools for not having said them before now."

Jared knew some other powerful words that they could exchange. Was this the right time? Did he want to hear them? Did he want to *say* them?

Yes.

"Emma . . ." He took another step toward her, but she nervously backed away. His heart sank. *Is it too late?*

"The gifts," she stuttered out. "What was Molly talking about when she mentioned gifts?"

Jared saw yearning in her eyes but also fear. She was afraid. Of what? Of him? Of making a mistake? Of laying her heart bare and being rejected? Those were the things making him afraid.

So, what was the worst thing that could happen? A

blow to his silly pride? Hadn't his pride stood in the way too long already? And if the worst didn't happen . . . if the best happened instead . . . he could have Emma back.

He wanted that more than anything else in the world.

Take a chance, Stapleton. Take a chance on yourself, Emma, and the love you've shared for so long. Reaching out, he took her hand. "I brought Christmas gifts for you, Emma."

She licked her lips. "You did?"

"Yep." His heart pounded, and he realized he was a little afraid, also. "I have this year's gift. And three more."

"Four. You brought last year's gift?"

He nodded. "And from the year before that. And, from that first awful year.

A ghost of a smile flashed over her lips. "I brought gifts for you, too."

He lifted her hand to his lips and kissed her knuckles. "You did?"

Her smile returned and stayed. "I also brought four."

"What are they?"

"It's not Christmas yet."

"Isn't it? I feel as if maybe Christmas has come early."

Jared pulled her into his arms, and she willingly melted against him. "I know some other powerful words that need to be said."

They spoke simultaneously.

"I love you, Jared Stapleton."

"I love you, Emma Stapleton."

They stared into each other's eyes, love shining bright enough to light up the cave. Then, with joy in his heart, Jared bent his head and claimed his wife's mouth in a long, passionate kiss beneath the mistletoe.

When they finally came up for air, Jared checked his watch. They had another hour before Molly said she'd return, and there was a handy stack of quilts on the shelf behind his wife. "Speaking of Christmas gifts, gonna let me unwrap mine now?"

A tiny frown creased Emma's brow. "They're back at Angel's Rest."

His fingers slipped a pearl button on her blouse free of its buttonhole. "Not all of them."

Emma's shiver had nothing to do with the cold.

Twinkle lights blinked on the twelve-foot fir tree that was the centerpiece of Christmas decorations in the downstairs parlor of Angel's Rest. Emma studied the ornaments—an angel-themed tree—and decided to get some angels for their Christmas tree at the Wildcatter.

A sound in the hallway caught her attention, and she turned to see her daughter wrapped in her fiancé's arms beneath the ball of mistletoe hanging from the light fixture. Gladness filled Emma's heart. When Jared's hand slipped around her waist, she glanced up with a smile. He, too, was looking at the couple in the hallway. "He's a lucky young man."

"The luckiest," Emma agreed.

"No." Jared squeezed her waist. "That would be me."

Emma fingered the angel-wings pendant hanging from a long silver chain around her neck, a gift from Celeste. The Angel's Rest blazon, she called it, signified the healing of a broken heart. "I think we're all lucky. I know that tonight I feel blessed."

Earlier, they had broken from strict Stapleton family tradition and opened their gifts. Now Mozart was upstairs in his travel crate, happily chewing on the toy Jared had given him while wearing the stylish new collar that was Molly's gift. Molly wore the diamond stud earrings that had been a gift from her parents.

Jared's gifts to Emma and her gifts to him remained wrapped up in their boxes, and they would stay that way. They'd both decided that, in this case, it truly was the thought that counted. Those wrapped packages would forever be symbols of their love that never died. The perfect Christmas gifts.

Outside, church bells began to peal. Molly and Mason broke their kiss, then Molly looked at her parents and smiled with utter joy. "Merry Christmas, parents."

"Merry Christmas, daughter and son," Jared replied.

Though Emma wouldn't have thought it possible, Molly's smile grew even brighter. "The human heart is a curious thing. How can it possibly hold this much joy?"

The grandfather clock in the hallway chimed the

quarter hour as Celeste descended the stairs, a vision in a shimmery gold dress with a white wool coat draped over her arm. "Merry Christmas, friends. I'm so glad you are joining us for our midnight service, especially since I just received a phone call from Kelly Green. We've had a bit of a problem, and we're hoping you will help."

And so it was that at eleven-thirty at night on Christmas Eve, with her daughter and her husband seated in the pew behind her, Emma Stapleton took a seat at the piano in St. Stephen's. The first song she played was "Joy to the World."

The congregation members agreed that the song had never been played so beautifully.

EXCERPT FROM THE CHRISTMAS PAWDCAST

Dallas, Texas

"Carol of the Bells" drifted from the sound system and blended with the laughter of the holiday party guests who were taking their leave. Mary Landry worked to keep the smile on her face as she hugged and cheek-kissed and waved goodbyes to the stragglers. She had enjoyed the party, and she was thrilled that so many invited guests had attended. But seriously, would these people never go home? She still had so much to do! How could it possibly already be December twentieth?

"Tonight was so much fun," bubbled a wedding planner from Plano, her blue eyes sparkling with champagne. "Landry and Lawrence Catering throws the best party of the season, year in and year out. Thanks so much for inviting us!"

"I'm so glad you could join us." Mary graciously accepted the woman's enthusiastic hug and glanced up at her date. "Shall I call an Uber for y'all?"

"We're good," he said. "I'm the designated driver tonight, but I can't say I missed the booze. Your non-alcoholic eggnog was killer."

"Mary is the best chef in Dallas," the wedding planner declared. "Restaurants are always trying to lure her into their kitchens."

"Mary! Great party!" A venue manager sailed toward them, which helped ease the first couple out the door. "I don't know what tweak you made to your mac-and-cheese recipe, but it made the exquisite simply divine."

She hadn't changed a thing. "Thank you, Liz."

"You gonna share your recipe?"

"Nope. Trade secrets."

"Dang it. Although my waistline and arteries both thank you for that. Merry Christmas, Mary."

"Merry Christmas."

Finally, almost an hour after the party had been scheduled to end, Mary's business partner Eliza Lawrence shut the door behind the last guest. She gave her long brown hair a toss and flourished her arms like a game show hostess. "We are so freaking awesome!"

Mary laughed. "Yes, we are."

"I do believe tonight even topped last year's party, which I didn't think would be possible."

"Everything went like clockwork—except getting guests to depart."

Eliza waved her hand dismissively. "That's the sign of a successful event. You know that."

Mary nodded. It was why their Christmas event was

the one party of the year where Eliza, the logistics director of their business, loosened her timeline.

"Everyone raved about the food as usual," Eliza continued, "but the shrimp balls were a particular hit. You outdid yourself with those, Mary. The vendors who were here tonight are going to talk them up to their clients. We'll be up to our elbows in shrimp all next year."

"I figured they'd be a hit. Nothing has topped my maple mac-and-cheese, though. I think that was all gone by nine o'clock."

"The Landry and Lawrence classic." Eliza sighed happily. "You ready for a glass of champagne? I built time for champagne into our schedule. The cleanup crew doesn't arrive for forty minutes."

"I'm more than ready." Mary's thoughts returned to her to-do list, and she winced. "Mind drinking it in my office? I need to finish my dad's gift before I head home tonight."

Eliza chastised her with a look.

"I know. I know."

Her partner reached out and gave Mary a quick hug. "I'll grab a bottle and glasses and meet you in your office on one condition."

Mary's mouth twisted in a crooked smile. "What's that?"

"Change your clothes before you break out the hot glue gun. I don't want to be taking you to the ER with third-degree boob burns five days before Christmas."

Mary snorted.

"I think I heard almost as many comments on how great you looked tonight as I heard about how fantastic the shrimp balls tasted. It's a spectacular dress, Mar. I'm glad you decided to show off your curves for a change. Emerald is your color. It brings out your eyes. I swear, when Travis arrived and got a look at you, I thought he was going to swallow his tongue."

"Because I'm wearing last year's Christmas gift." Mary fingered the teardrop garnet pendant that nestled against her breasts. "He accidentally left it off the list of things he asked me to return when he dumped me."

Eliza wrinkled her nose. "If I said it once, I said it a thousand times. The man is a dewsh. I know we couldn't cut him from the guest list because he does own three wedding venues in the Metroplex, but I honestly didn't think he'd have the nerve to show up with her in tow."

"Oh, I knew they'd be here." That's why she'd made such an effort with her outfit tonight.

"Well, you definitely won tonight's skirmish. Raylene sailed in here dressed in her slinky silver sequins, holding her nose in the air and flashing her rock, but you put her in her place without so much as a 'Bless your heart,' just by being gracious."

"She's a beautiful woman."

"And you're a natural red-headed pagan goddess—who will find somebody worthy of you. Trust me, you dodged a bullet by getting rid of that creep."

Emotion closed Mary's throat, and tears stung her eyes. How was it that Eliza always knew just the right thing to say? While she'd put Travis Trent behind her, and she hadn't cried over him in over five months, seeing him tonight hadn't been easy. No woman enjoyed seeing her ex parade her replacement around in front of her. Especially not in her own place of business. Clearing her throat, Mary tried to lighten the subject by saying, "I was aiming for sexy Santa's helper."

"Honey, I wouldn't be surprised to find a dozen men in red suits and white beards lined up outside our door when we leave here tonight."

Mary laughed. What would she do without her best friend? "Oh, Eliza. I do love you."

"I love you, too. Now go cover up that fabulous rack so you can finish your dad's gift. I'm going to change, too, and then I'll grab the bubbly and meet you in your office."

Ten minutes later, armed with a hot glue gun and wearing jeans, a sweatshirt, and her favorite sneakers, Mary put the finishing touches on the Daddy-Daughter scrapbook she'd made for her father. It had long been a Landry family tradition between her parents and two siblings to exchange handmade gifts at Christmas. With her brother and sister both married, the practice had expanded to include spouses and Mary's two nephews and three nieces. Of course, she bought the little ones toys, too, but handmade gifts where the ones that mattered for the adults.

Eliza strolled into her office, carrying two crystal flutes in her right hand and a green bottle in her left. She set the glasses on Mary's desk and went about the business of opening the champagne. "Sorry I took so long.

John called to grovel about missing the party, so I let him do it even though I totally support his job. I knew what I was in for when I fell for an obstetrician."

"Did his patient have her babies?"

"She did. Mama and triplets are doing great."

"Excellent."

Eliza filled two glasses with the sparkling wine, handed one to Mary, then raised her glass in a toast. "Merry Christmas, BFF."

"Merry Christmas. I hope you and John have a fabulous time in Hawaii."

"How can we not? Ten days of sun and sand, just the two of us, totally unplugged? It'll be heaven."

"The unplugged part sounds like heaven," Mary agreed.

"You're such a traditionalist, Mary."

"And unapologetic about it. For me, Christmas wouldn't be Christmas without all the trappings. I want family around me, bubble lights on the tree, and carols on the sound system. I want cookies to decorate and big fluffy bows on gifts. I want midnight mass and hot apple cider and 'It's a Wonderful Life' and sleigh rides. And I want snow!"

Eliza clinked her glass with Mary's. "And this is the difference between a girl born and raised in south Texas and one who grew up in the Rocky Mountains. So, when are you planning to leave for Colorado?"

"With any luck, first thing tomorrow morning." Mary sipped her champagne, then set it down. She checked the finishing touch on the scrapbook with her fingertip. The miniature fishing creel placed at the corner of a twenty-year-old photo of her father fishing with his three children in Rocky Mountain National Park was nice and dry. It was safe to close the book. Mary needed to wrap it and the two hardcover novels containing the handmade gift IOU's she was giving her brother and sister before she headed home. Her sibs understood her busy season and would be happy with better-late-than-never, thank goodness.

"In other good news, I finally found a dog sitter for Angel. Jason Elliott told me tonight he'd take her. He just needs to clear it with his roommate. He said he'd call me tonight if there was a problem, and my phone hasn't rung."

On cue, Mary's cell phone rang.

It lay pushed to the side of her desk in its seasonal decorative Santa case. Her ring tone of choice for December was "White Christmas," and for the first time in Mary's life, the sound of Bing Crosby's voice didn't make her happy. She closed her eyes and whimpered a little as she reached to answer. "Hello?"

Two and a half minutes later, she disconnected the call, buried her head in her hands, and groaned.

Eliza set a champagne flute in front of her. "No room at Jason's inn, either, I take it?"

"No. Jason was my last hope. There's no other option. I've called every vet, every boarding facility, pet hotel, and pet sitter within fifty miles. Everything is full and has a waitlist. Nobody is offering me any hope that Angel will find a bed for Christmas."

Eliza winced. She took a sip of her drink and then pursed her lips and pondered a moment. "You asked Sarah?"

"Yes. And Linda, April, José, Kiley, Kenisha, Sam, Father Tom, Reverend Jenkins, Officer Larimer…"

"The butcher, the baker, and the candlestick maker?"

"Them, too."

"I'm sorry, sweets. You'd know I'd help if John and I weren't leaving for Hawaii tomorrow. I suppose it wouldn't be kind of me to say I told you so when you said yes to Wags and Walks?"

Mary chastised her partner with a look.

Eliza lifted her champagne in a toast. "Honey, you know I love dogs as much as anybody, and I think the work you do for Wags and Walks Rescue qualifies you for sainthood. But that dog…"

"She's an angel," Mary defended. "She's aptly named."

"Unfortunately, people aren't any different about choosing their pets than they are about choosing their partners. I'm afraid you might be stuck with that dog for a long time. Appearance matters. Note that you didn't choose to name her "Beauty" when the other volunteer pulled her from the pound and then dumped her on you at the last minute."

Mary brought her chin up. "Beauty is in the eyes of the beholder. Angel's forever family will see past her… challenges…to her sweet personality. I simply haven't had time to find them. Besides, it's not like I didn't know that I was taking on a special case when I let Rhonda Blankenship leave her with me."

"I know. I know. But I also witnessed your call to the rescue director. I heard her swear on her mother's grave that she would find a dog sitter over Christmas if you agreed to step in for Rhonda and take the new dog."

Mary shrugged. "Things happen."

"Right. And women elope and bail on commitments at the last minute all the time. So where did Rhonda and her new husband move to again?"

"Yap. It's an island in the South Pacific. It's supposed to be beautiful."

Eliza rolled her eyes and drawled, "I hope they'll be very happy. So that's it, then? You have no choice but to take that poor, pitiful, diarrhetic dog with you on a four-teen-hour car trip, then foist her off on your parents for two weeks? They're going to love that."

"They won't mind. Much. They're both dog lovers, although Mom does prefer little dogs."

"Nothing about Angel is little. She's a horse. A big, hairy horse."

"She's a big dog, yes, but don't forget she's carrying extra weight."

"I don't see how, considering that she tosses her cookies every time she eats. Oh, Mary. I'm going to worry about your road-warrioring in a seen-better-days Ford uphill through the blizzard with only a big, ugly, sick dog for company."

Mary gave her friend a chastising look. "Number one, my car might have a lot of miles, but it runs like a champ. Number two, I'm going to pretend I didn't hear the U-word. Number three, I've checked the travel conditions between Dallas and Eternity Springs, and nobody is predicting a blizzard to hit in the next two days. It's two to four inches of snow at the most once I reach the mountains, and I'll most likely be home before it starts. Number four, Angel isn't sick. The pregnancy has given her a sensitive digestive system. And finally, number five, I forbid you to spend one minute thinking about me, much less worrying. I expect you to devote all your time and attention to wringing every bit of comfort and joy from your romantic Christmas vacation with Dr. Hottie. And, to assist in that endeavor, I have a little something for you."

Mary opened one of her desk drawers and removed the small, wrapped package she'd placed there earlier.

"Mary!" Eliza exclaimed. "We already exchanged gifts. I love, love, love, love the organizer you gave me."

"I'm glad. This is a little something extra. It's my heart gift."

Eliza's eyes widened. Her voice held a note of wonder as she accepted the box, saying, "But…you didn't have time this year. You've only just finished your dad's gift. You're giving your siblings IOU's. You didn't even have time for the big fat family tradition event that's so important to you, your 'Gift of Giving to a Stranger.' But you took the time to make something for me?"

Mary could have pointed out how Eliza never

failed to be there for her during the breakup with Travis. She could have talked about their excellent working relationship or the way Eliza always made her laugh when Mary really needed a laugh. But instead, she simply said, "You're my best friend, Eliza."

Her best friend burst out in uncharacteristic tears and tore into her present. "Booties! You knitted booties for me!"

"For the plane ride."

"Because I always kick my shoes off, and my feet always freeze. They're so soft. They're like a turquoise cloud. They're perfect. Thank you, Mary. I love them." Eliza threw her arms around her friend and gave her a hard hug. "There's only one problem. No way I won't think about you when I'm wearing them."

"Fair enough. You have permission to think about me only while you're sitting in First Class, wearing my booties, and sipping a Mai Tai."

"It's a deal. I'll drink a toast to you and Angel and tap my turquoise heels three times and wish you safely home over the river and through the woods without encountering a tornado or a blizzard or a cat named Toto."

"No cats. Angel doesn't care for cats."

Both women turned at the sound of the loading dock's buzzer. The cleanup crew had arrived. Eliza took one last sip of her champagne and set down the flute. "I've got the afterparty. Consider it my heart gift to you. Stay here and wrap your presents, then go home and get a good night's sleep so that you and Angel can get an early start in the morning."

Mary accepted the gift in the spirit it was offered, and she gave her friend one more hug. "Thank you. Merry Christmas, Eliza."

"Merry Christmas, Mary." Booties in hand and whistling "I Saw Mommy Kissing Santa Claus," she left the office. A minute later, she ducked back inside and tossed something toward Mary, saying, "Since you're so big on Christmas traditions, I think you should stick this in your purse."

Jingle bells jangled as Mary caught the red ribbon holding the sprig of mistletoe that had been part of their decoration.

Eliza said, "You want to be the Girl Scout Elf when you're out walking Angel and run into Santa Hunk. Always prepared, you know."

"Santa Hunk?

"I know you are spending Christmas in a small, isolated town with a shortage of single guys, but hey, it's the season of miracles, right? Put it in your purse, Mary."

Mary laughed, did as she was told, then returned to her gift wrapping. She finished up quickly. After checking with her partner, who assured her that everything was under control, she headed home to bed.

Mary dreamed vividly that night. Snow swirled in peppermint scented air, but there were no clouds in the inky blue sky, only a full moon and a million stars. She was flying. She was flying in a sleigh pulled by reindeer

—with Angel in Rudolf's lead position. Angel's nose glowed red, and around her neck hung a St. Bernard's cask of brandy. Bing Crosby crooned about a white Christmas from the sleigh's sound system speakers.

Mary wore her green Christmas party dress, a red felt hat with jingle bells and pointed tip, and sparkling Judy Garland ruby slippers with curled, pointy toes. Was the curl because they were elf shoes, or because mistletoe hung above the sleigh, and Santa Hunk had kissed her all across the Pacific?

When the sleigh sailed past an airliner headed toward Hawaii, she came up for air long enough to give Eliza a beauty queen wave. Eliza lifted her Mai Tai in a toast.

Mary awoke with a smile on her face.

As a rule, she wasn't one to put any stock in the notion that dreams foretold the future. Still, right before she backed her loaded-up eight-year-old Ford Explorer out of the driveway, she added a new song to her playlist for the trip.

Mary Landry headed home to Eternity Springs, Colorado, for Christmas, singing along to "Santa Baby."

Order THE CHRISTMAS PAWDCAST today.

AUTHOR'S NOTE

In the Eternity Springs timeline, MISTLETOE MINE takes place after HEARTACHE FALLS and before LOVER'S LEAP.

Sign up for Emily's newsletter to receive news about upcoming books, special sales, and contests at www.emilymarch.com/newsletter

ALSO BY EMILY MARCH

MIRACLE ROAD

DREAMWEAVER TRAIL

TEARDROP LANE

HEARTSONG COTTAGE

REUNION PASS

CHRISTMAS IN ETERNITY SPRINGS

A STARDANCE SUMMER

THE FIRST KISS OF SPRING

THE CHRISTMAS WISHING TREE

The *Eternity Springs: McBrides of Texas Trilogy*

JACKSON

TUCKER

BOONE

***Celebrate Eternity Springs* Novella Collection**

THE CHRISTMAS PAWDCAST novella

BETTER THAN A BOX OF CHOCOLATES novella

THE SUMMER MELT novella

And, SEASON OF SISTERS, a stand alone women's fiction novel.

The Bad Luck Wedding Historical Romance Series

THE BAD LUCK WEDDING DRESS

THE BAD LUCK WEDDING CAKE

ABOUT THE AUTHOR

Emily March is the *New York Times, Publishers Weekly*, and *USA Today* bestselling author of over forty novels, including the critically acclaimed Eternity Springs series. Publishers Weekly calls March a "master of delightful banter," and her heartwarming, emotionally charged stories have been named to Best of the Year lists by *Publishers Weekly, Library Journal,* and Romance Writers of America.

A graduate of Texas A&M University, Emily is an avid fan of Aggie sports and her recipe for jalapeño relish has made her a tailgating legend.

Made in United States
North Haven, CT
09 October 2023

42569484R00071